英語 Make Me High 系列

三版

關鍵句型100
Key Sentence Structures 100

郭慧敏 編著

三民書局

序

英語 Make Me High 系列的理想在於超越，在於創新。

這是時代的精神，也是我們出版的動力；

這是教育的目的，也是我們進步的執著。

針對英語的全球化與未來的升學趨勢，

我們設計了一系列適合普高、技高學生的英語學習書籍。

面對英語，不會徬徨不再迷惘，學習的心徹底沸騰，

心情好 High！

實戰模擬，掌握先機知己知彼，百戰不殆決勝未來，

分數更 High！

選擇優質的英語學習書籍，才能激發學習的強烈動機；

興趣盎然便不會畏懼艱難，自信心要自己大聲說出來。

本書如良師指引循循善誘，如益友相互鼓勵攜手成長。

展書輕閱，你將發現……

學習英語原來也可以這麼 High！

再版序

　　本書於 2004 年出版至今廣受好評，期間我們也得到許多建議與指教，於是決定進行改版的動作。此次改版，做了多方面的考量與決策，其目的無非是為了幫助莘莘學子們在閱讀此教材時，能在最短的時間內吸收最豐富的英文資訊。

　　為了實現「以最簡單的模式加深最深刻印象」的旨意，書中的句型以提示關鍵字的形式標示，簡化了複雜刻板的句型公式，再輔以詳細的用法說明，使同學們不必再背誦抽象的句型公式，也讓老師不須再為了如何解釋句型公式而苦惱。此外，條列代表性句型仍是最新版中的一大特色，如在提到獨立分詞構句時，以最具代表性及使用率最頻繁的 frankly speaking 作為條列的句型，而在用法說明時，再一一列出其他常見的獨立分詞構句，以使讀者能更加熟悉其句型；或是在介紹假設語氣用法之一的句型時，列出最基本且具提示性的句型 If...should...，並在說明時詳述關於此假設句型在文法與意義上更深入的用法，以使讀者能更融會貫通。因此在最新版本中，用法說明將較前一版本更加詳實精確。

　　在英文的領域中，文法、片語、慣用語與句型四者密不可分。有鑑於此，《關鍵句型 100》囊括了最關鍵、常用的句型，並補充許多常見於各大考中的片語與慣用語於「學習補給站」之中，其中囊括了和主要句型在「形」或「義」上相似的其他句型與片語於內，以期讀者能更詳加分辨及了解其他相關用法；希望同學們在學習英文句型的過程中，除了能夠貫通文法概念之外，也能夠活用片語與慣用語。

　　最新版的《關鍵句型 100》中，我們保留了前一版本的精華之處，並針對前一版本的說明文字稍作調整，以深入淺出的方式來介紹句型概念；另外，我們在書中增加了許多重要及實用的資訊，期望能與老師和同學們一起輕鬆學習關鍵，輕鬆面對考試。

郭慧敏於中和高中

March, 2006

作者序

　　最近幾年英語教育中所重視的溝通式教學法 (communicative approach)，課程中強調任務導向學習 (task-based learning) 及問題導向學習 (problem-based learning)，乃至於資訊融入教學所期盼的專題式導向學習 (project-based learning)，都大大地提昇了本島學生的英文表現。這種進步我稱之為「跳躍式的進步」，也就是在資源分配不均、經濟落差太大之下，即便是民間版本教課書日趨成熟完整，教學資源日益完備，反而在學測等大考評量的結果中產生「雙峰現象」。事實上，身為第一線的教師，一則以喜，一則以憂：喜的是學生的聽說能力在多元文化刺激之下，(包括西洋電影、歌曲的接觸，以及網路資訊的接收)，較之於以往學生的表現優秀，所以在課堂上要進入全英語教學的環境已經非完全不可能。憂的是學生習慣於動口，卻拙於動手，換言之，學生的學習行為模式已經改變，所呈現出來的學習表現很難在筆試中得到掌聲。最大的弱點就在拼字正確度的掌控力很低，句子表達力的完整性欠缺，特別是不重視基本文法，往往一個簡單的句子就可能拼錯 2 到 3 個字，或錯用片語，或文法上的瑕疵比比皆是。

　　面對學測等大考時，我的學生常在徬徨時會問我：「老師，該怎麼準備英文？要讀課本嗎？為什麼考題和課本所教的似乎都沒有關係？」我常對我的學生們說：「準備英文考試與其他學科最大的不同點就是無法用章節逐一檢視自己的學習成果。」考前三個月要開始進入統整戰鬥力的磨練：

第一步是基本功操練：

(1)字彙每日向前推進 15 到 30 頁 (讀完做題目則每日 15 頁，若不做題目則每日 30 頁)。

(2)片語每日向前推進 1 單元或 2 單元 (讀完做題目則每日 1 單元，若不做題目則每日 2 單元)。

(3)句型每日向前推進 2 到 4 個 (讀完做題目則每日 2 個，若不做題目則每日 4 個)。

第二步是單兵作戰演練：

(1)每日做一大題：或字彙片語 15 題、或克漏字 15 題、或文意選填 10 題、或閱讀測驗 2 篇、或翻譯題 5 題，認真做完務必仔細看詳解，將不會的問題當日解決。記住：做題目在「精」不在「多」。

(2)每週做一份完整的模擬試題，前 5 份包括作文給自己 70 分鐘的時間完成，6–10 份強迫自己 65 分鐘完成，最後幾份要壓縮到 60 分鐘之內完成，認真做完後務必仔細對照詳解，充分了解自己的錯誤並訂正。記住：請挑下午 2 點至 3 點半做模擬試題，調整生理及心理的狀態，屆時能完全適應情境。

筆者於前年完成《7000 字彙速成》，去年完成《關鍵片語 800》，今年決定介紹《關鍵句型 100》，意在幫助學生操練基本功時能有所本，面對考試的壓力時不再驚慌，要相信自己距離成功只差那一步，而關鍵的一步就在於「相信自己會成功」。在此祝福每一位面對考試的學子，在關鍵時刻做出關鍵的抉擇，你一定會有關鍵性的突破。

郭慧敏於永和家中

June 15, 2004

Table of Contents

Unit 1   與 it 有關的句型   *1*

Unit 2   與代名詞有關的句型   *11*

Unit 3   與助動詞有關的句型   *19*

Unit 4   與不定詞有關的句型   *27*

Unit 5   與分詞有關的句型   *43*

Unit 6   與動名詞有關的句型   *53*

Unit 7   與關係詞有關的句型   *65*

Unit 8   與時間有關的句型   *75*

Unit 9   與假設或條件有關的句型   *83*

Unit 10   與比較有關的句型   *95*

Unit 11   與否定有關的句型   *113*

Unit 12   與讓步有關的句型   *121*

Unit 13   與目的、程度、結果有關的句型   *129*

Unit 14   特殊句型   *139*

解答   *149*

索引   *166*

本書圖片來源：Shutterstock

Unit 1　　與 it 有關的句型

1　　It is...for...to V

It is important **for us to learn** how to deal with emergencies.

(對我們來說，學習要如何處理緊急事故是重要的。)

用法說明

1　本句型的 It 為虛主詞，之後的不定詞才是真正的主詞。

2　此種句型中，用於修飾事物常見的形容詞有：easy (容易的)、difficult (困難的)、natural (自然的)、dangerous (危險的)、necessary (必需的)、possible (可能的)、convenient (方便的)、important (重要的) 等字。

　　· It is *dangerous* for a child to walk alone in a dark alley.

　　　(對一個小孩來說，獨自在暗巷中行走是危險的。)

3　若使用的形容詞可修飾人的特質，如 kind (仁慈的)、wise (明智的)、clever (聰明的)、foolish (愚笨的)、cruel (殘酷的)、polite (有禮貌的)、careful (小心的)、generous (慷慨的)、honest (誠實的) 等字，則句型中的介系詞以 of 替換，其句型為：It is...of...to V。

　　· It is *generous* of you to finance me. (你真慷慨能在財務上資助我。)

4　可代換之句型：

　　· It is important for us to learn how to deal with emergencies.

　　　→ It is important that we learn how to deal with emergencies.

　　· It is generous of you to finance me.

　　　→ You are generous to finance me.

超級比一比

> It was wrong <u>for</u> you to cheat on the exam.
>
> (指「作弊」一事是不對的) (你考試作弊,那是不對的。)
>
> It was wrong <u>of</u> you to cheat on the exam.
>
> (強調「你」的行為是不對的) (你考試作弊是不對的。)

學習補給站

★ **It is no use + V-ing**　…是沒有用的 (參考 **36** 學習補給站)

It 在此句型中亦是虛主詞,替代 V-ing。

- <u>It is no use crying</u> over spilt milk.

  → Crying over spilt milk is no use. (【諺】覆水難收。)

關鍵試航

1. 我們可能會遲到。(possible)

   _____

2. Tony 的隊伍要贏得比賽是輕而易舉的。(easy)

   _____

3. 警方這麼做太蠢了。(foolish)

   _____

4. 與我們的父母爭執是沒有用的。(use)

   _____

2　find it + <u>Adj/N</u> + to V

I found it interesting **to talk with** a man like him.

(我發現和像他一樣的人談話很有趣。)

用法說明

1 find 為不完全及物動詞，故後除接受詞 (it) 外，還需加上受詞補語 (Adj/N) 使語意完整，其他類似用法的動詞有：consider (認為)、make (使成為)、think (想)、believe (相信)、feel (覺得) 等字。

・ I <u>thought it</u> my duty <u>to guard</u> my country. (我認為保衛國家是我的責任。)

2 本句型中，it 用來代替後面的不定詞片語，而不定詞片語才是真正的受詞。it 也可以代替由 that、whether、how、why、when 所引導的子句。

・ I believe it true <u>that they are siblings.</u> (我相信他們真的是手足。)

3 不定詞片語之前亦可加入 for + 人，其句型為：不完全及物動詞 + it...for + 人 + to V。

・ What <u>makes it difficult for you to tell</u> the truth? (是什麼事情讓你難以說出實話？)

學習補給站

★ **make it a rule to V**　習慣於…

此片語為固定用法，it 指的是後面的不定詞片語。

・ She <u>makes it a rule to eat</u> something before going to bed.

(她習慣在睡前吃一點東西。)

★ **take it for granted that...**　視…為理所當然

此片語亦為固定用法，it 指的是後面 that 所引導的名詞子句。

・ Children often <u>take it for granted that</u> their parents should give them anything they want. (孩子們常常認為父母理應給他們想要的一切。)

關鍵試航

1. 我發覺要及時完成 (complete) 工作是不可能的。

_____

2. 我們都覺得你離開公司是一件可惜的事 (a pity)。

_____

3. 惡劣的天氣使登山者們難以抵達山頂。(make it hard)

_____

4. 我爸爸習慣早睡早起。(make it a rule)

_____

5. 我認為 Jones 博士準時出席會議是理所當然的。(take it for granted that)

_____

3 It seems/appears that...

It seems/appears that a typhoon is approaching.

(颱風似乎快來了。)

用法說明

1 本句型與 seem/appear + to V 可互相代換，但須特別注意 seem 和 appear 與 that 子句中動詞的時態：

(1)動詞時態相同時，seem/appear to 之後接原形動詞。

· It seems that Sue likes pizza very much.

→ Sue seems to like pizza very much. (Sue 似乎很喜歡披薩。)

(2)動詞時態不同時 (that 子句中的動作較早發生)，seem/appear to 之後接 have + V-en。(參考 **20 seem to have + V-en**)

· It seems that Andy was handsome when he was young.

→ Andy seems to have been handsome when he was young.

(Andy 年輕時似乎很英俊。)

2 其他類似用法的句型尚有：

★ **It is said that...**　據說⋯

· It is said that he was brave and tough.

→ He is said to have been brave and tough. (據說他曾經是勇敢且堅強的。)

學習補給站

★ **It follows that...**　結果是⋯

· According to the current evidence, it follows that he is the suspect.

(根據目前的證據顯示，他就是嫌疑犯。)

★ **It goes without saying that...** 　不用說；無庸置疑地

- It goes without saying that honesty is the best policy.

　(無庸置疑地，誠實為上策。)

關鍵試航

1. 你和我在一起似乎一點也不快樂。

_____

2. 你似乎完全錯了。

_____

3. 我們的經理似乎對那件洋裝很滿意。

_____

4. 據說這位老先生以前是個百萬富翁。

_____

4　It takes...to V

It took ten years **to complete** the MRT system.

(完成捷運系統花了十年的時間。)

用法說明

1 若要表示某人花時間去做某件事情，take 之後可接人與時間再接不定詞片語，即：

It takes + 人 + 時間 + to V。

- It took *the firefighters ten minutes* to unlock the door.

　(消防隊員花了十分鐘才打開門。)

2 除了花費時間之外，take 之後還可接 patience 或 courage，表達做某事需要耐心或勇氣。

- It takes *patience* to take care of the elderly who are sick. (照顧生病的長者需要耐心。)
- It takes *great courage* to face the music. (面對現實需要極大的勇氣。)

3 此句型的原問句為詢問做某動作需費時多久，句型為：

How long does it take to V?　做某事需要多久的時間？

- How long does it take to get there by bus? (搭公車到那裡需要多久時間？)

4 如果要表示花費金額，則將動詞 take 改為 cost，即：It costs + 人 + 費用 + to V。

- It cost *me one hundred bucks* to have my hair cut. (我花了一百元剪頭髮。)

關鍵試航

1. 建這座橋花了三年的時間。

___

2. 實現他的夢想花了他一生的時間。

___

3. 我花了五百元把電腦修好。

___

4. 訓練這些動物需要極大的耐心。

___

5. 公開演講需要一些勇氣。

___

5 It occurs to ＋ sb ＋ that...

It never occurred to me that the singer would end up in jail.

(我從未想到這位歌手的下場竟是坐牢。)

用法說明

1 此句型的 It 是虛主詞，真正的主詞是後面的 that 子句。It 所指的是 that 子句中所提到的內容。

- It occurred to him that he forgot to turn off the light when he left home.

  (他突然想起出門時忘了關燈。)

2 occur 在本句型中為表達某一想法突然浮現在腦中，無被動型態，且主詞不會是人。occur 為不及物動詞，後接受詞時須先加上介系詞 to。

3 與其同義的另一句型為：It strikes ＋ sb ＋ that...，strike 為及物動詞，所以受詞之前沒有介系詞。

· It struck me that our French teacher might get sick.

(我突然想到我們的法文老師可能生病了。)

關鍵試航

1. 我們從未想過他居然會說謊。(occur)

2. 我突然想到我應該馬上打個電話給我父母。(occur)

3. Fred 突然想起他應該保守秘密。(strike)

6　It doesn't matter...whether...

It doesn't matter to me **whether** you help me or not.

(你是否幫我對我而言並不重要。)

用法說明

1 It 在此句型中仍是虛主詞的用法，真正的主詞是後面由 whether 所引導的名詞子句。matter 是不及物動詞，表「重要，要緊」之意。

2 此句型大都以否定句或疑問句的形式出現，常與 not、never 或 little 並用。

· It never matters much to my brother whether he earns much money or not.
(錢賺得多或少對我弟弟而言無關緊要。)

· It matters little whether you are overweight or not. (你是否過重不是那麼重要。)

· Does it matter whether we win in the end? (我們最後是否獲勝重要嗎？)

3 whether 子句也可用 if 子句替換。

· It doesn't matter if you have time to join us for dinner.
(你是否有時間與我們共進晚餐並不重要。)

學習補給站

★ **It makes no difference whether...** ⋯沒什麼差別

- It makes no difference whether you add sugar or syrup to the coffee.

(你在咖啡裡加入糖或糖漿沒有什麼差別。)

關鍵試航

1. 教練是否會出現對參賽者們而言無關緊要。

_____

2. 你是否贊成我的提案不是那麼重要。(little)

_____

3. 她是否為總統的女兒對我而言幾乎不重要。(hardly)

_____

4. 結果是好或壞並不重要。

_____

5. 你去上學或去上班對我而言沒什麼差別。

_____

7 It is...that... (強調句)

It was out of curiosity **that** he went into that house.

(是好奇心驅使讓他走進那棟房子。)

用法說明

1 本句型可分別用來強調句中的主詞、受詞及副詞。

- Peter broke the vase yesterday. (Peter 昨天打破花瓶。)

  主詞　　受詞　副詞

  → It was Peter that broke the vase yesterday. (強調是 Peter 這個人打破的)

  → It was the vase that Peter broke yesterday. (強調打破的是 the vase)

  → It was yesterday that Peter broke the vase. (強調是在 yesterday 打破的)

2 本強調句所強調的副詞可以是片語，也可以是子句。

- It was <u>on the sixth of May</u> that Joseph was born.

  (Joseph 是在五月六日出生的。)

- It is <u>because I love the cartoon very much</u> that I bought the puppet.

  (就是因為我很喜歡這部卡通影片，我才會買這個玩偶。)

3 若所強調的名詞為人時，則 that 可以用 who 替代，若所強調的名詞為物時，則 that 可以用 which 替代。

- It is a man of letters <u>who</u> I respect most. (有文采的人最受到我的尊敬。)

- It was the terrible noise <u>which</u> scared the child. (嚇壞孩子的是可怕的噪音。)

4 如果所強調的是疑問句，則可用下列句型來表達：疑問詞 ＋ <u>is</u>/<u>was</u> it that...?

- Who took the dictionary without my permission?

  → <u>Who was it that</u> took the dictionary without my permission?

  (是誰未經我的許可就拿走了字典？)

關鍵試航

1. 錯的人是 Mary。

_____

2. 他是在上個週末前往美國的。

_____

3. 這名女舞者因為感染 (come down with) 了流感，所以失去了贏得第一名的機會。

_____

4. 是你老闆出的價格讓我嚇一跳。(which)

_____

5. 王醫師正在著手進行什麼事？

_____

Exercises

I. *Fill a proper word in each of the following blanks.*

1. It is said that my English teacher was an athlete when he was young.

   → My English teacher _____ _____ _____ _____

   _____ an athlete when he was young.

2. Needless to say, the guy is handsome.

   → It goes _____ _____ _____ the guy is handsome.

3. I have difficulty reaching the goal.

   → I find _____ difficult to reach the goal.

II. *Choose one proper answer.*

_____ 1. It is _____ that should be to blame.

   (A) my   (B) me   (C) him   (D) he

_____ 2. I found _____ impossible to refuse my best friend's invitation.

   (A) that   (B) it   (C) them   (D) which

_____ 3. I consider it _____ to join the basketball team.

   (A) honorable   (B) honorably   (C) honors   (D) honored

_____ 4. Jet engines made _____ possible for planes to fly faster.

   (A) he   (B) that   (C) it   (D) one

_____ 5. _____ is likely that the company will succeed.

   (A) That   (B) This   (C) It   (D) Which

_____ 6. I think _____ better to do what he insisted.

   (A) that   (B) far   (C) had   (D) it

_____ 7. It is the lifeguard _____ saved the girl's life.

   (A) what   (B) which   (C) when   (D) who

_____ 8. Some students found it easy _____ English as a foreign language.

   (A) to learn   (B) learning   (C) learned   (D) to be learned

_____ 9. _____ will do you good to take some exercise every morning.

   (A) It   (B) There   (C) Those   (D) These

_____ 10. _____ seems that Judy forgot to lock the car.

   (A) That   (B) This   (C) What   (D) It

Unit 2　與代名詞有關的句型

8　one..., and the other...

I have two uncles. **One** lives in Japan, **and the other** lives in the U.S.A.

(我有兩個叔叔。一個住在日本，另一個住在美國。)

用法說明

1 本句型須用於句中有兩個人或兩件事物的情況，因此 two 或 both 等有「二」之意的字詞常出現在此句型或其上下文中。

　　· I hold a pen in one hand and a ruler in the other. (我一手握筆，另一手拿尺。)

2 如果 the other 改為複數 the others，此句型 one..., and the others... 須用於有三個以上指涉詞的句子之中，說明有一者是該情況，其餘的為另一種情況。而此時的 the others 就等於 the rest。

　　· He has five children. One is studying abroad, and the others are studying at home.

　　　→ He has five children. One is studying abroad, and the rest are studying at home.

　　　　(他有五個孩子。一個在國外讀書，其餘的都在國內。)

關鍵試航

1.我有兩個姊姊。一個讀大學，另一個讀高中。

_____

2.只有一個學生通過考試，其餘的都不及格。

_____

9　the one..., and the other...

Both health and wealth mean a lot to me. **The one** gives me happiness, **and the other** much enjoyment.

(健康與財富兩者對我意義皆重大。前者給我幸福，後者給我許多樂趣。)

用法說明

1 本句型的使用常見於比較性的段落中，用來補充說明兩個人或兩件事物，注意 the one 或 the other 指的都是單數名詞，故須搭配單數動詞。

2 另一同義片語：the former..., the latter... 亦表「前者…後者…」之意。但 the former 及 the latter 要視其所代替的名詞來決定單複數，如下面例句中代替的分別是 health 與 wealth，故動詞用的是單數 is。

　　• Health is above wealth. In other words, the former *is* more important than the latter.
　　　(健康勝於財富；換言之，前者比後者重要。)

3 that...this... 亦表「前者…後者…」之意，代替單數名詞，故搭配的動詞一定是單數形，特別注意 that 指的是前者，this 是後者。(that 指的是前句中的較遠者，也就是前者；this 指較近者，即後者。)

　　• I prefer tea to coffee; that *tastes* better than this.
　　　(我喜歡茶勝於咖啡，前者比後者好喝。)

4 those...these... 亦表「前者…後者…」之意，理論和 that...this... 相同，但用於代替複數名詞，故搭配的動詞一定是複數形，特別注意 those 指的是前者，these 是後者。

　　• I like dogs better than cats; those *are* more loyal than these.
　　　(我較喜歡狗而較不喜歡貓，前者比後者忠心。)

關鍵試航

1. 工作與玩樂都有必要；前者提供成就，後者提供休息。(the one..., and the other)

_____

_____

2. scene 和 scenery 都是指美麗的風景；前者是可數名詞，後者是不可數名詞。
　 (the former...the latter)

_____

_____

3. 你到高雄可以搭飛機或火車，但前者比後者快很多。(that...this)

_____

_____

10　some…, and/but others…

Some people like the pop singer's new album, **but others** don't.
(有些人喜歡這位流行歌手的新專輯，但有些人不喜歡。)

用法說明

1 在不特定的多數當中，若要對比其中兩類狀況，即可以使用此句型。又 other 只能用來代替可數名詞，所以若比較的事物為不可數名詞，則須把 others 改為 some。

- Some luggage has been put into the car, but some hasn't.
  (有些行李已經被放進車子裡了，但有些還沒。)

2 若對比的是限定範圍內之事物，則 others 之前須加上冠詞 the，用來特指限定範圍內剩下的那一些。

- There are many students in the library. Some are sleeping, and all the others are reading. (圖書館裡有許多學生，有一些在睡覺，其他的全都在看書。)

學習補給站

如果出現三者，要分別加以說明時，可以使用以下的句型：

one…another…the other…　　一個…另一個…第三個…

- I have three net pals. One is from French, another is from Spain, and the other is from Brazil.
  (我有三個網友。一個法國人，另一個西班牙人，第三個是巴西人。)

如果第三者為複數形，則用以下句型：

one…another…the others…　　一個…另一個…其餘的…

- Tony keeps many pets. One is a turtle, another is a mini pig, and the others are dogs.
  (Tony 養了許多寵物。一隻烏龜，一隻迷你豬，其餘都是狗。)

關鍵試航

1.公園裡有許多小孩。有些在放風箏，有些在騎腳踏車。

_____

_____

2. 有些金屬是磁性的，有些則不足。

_____

3. 體育館 (gym) 裡有許多學生。一些在打籃球，其餘的都在打桌球。

_____

_____

4. 他有三支手機。一支是紅的，一支是黑的，還有一支是銀的。

_____

_____

5. 有些食物好吃，有些不好吃。

_____

11　...is one thing, and...is another

To say **is one thing, and** to do **is another**.

(說是一回事，做又是另一回事。)

用法說明

1 此句型用於說明兩件不一樣的事情，可以代換為句型：...and...are two different things 或句型：...is different from...。

- Saying is one thing, and doing is another.
    - → Saying and doing are two different things.
    - → Saying is different from doing. (說是一回事，做又是一回事。)

2 若在 another 之前加上 quite 一字，則為強調語氣的用法。

- It is one thing to be in possession of wealth, and it is quite another to make good use of it. (擁有財富是一回事，而善用財富又是另一回事。)

學習補給站

★ **one another**　　(兩者或兩者以上) 彼此

- The students shook hands with one another. (學生們彼此握手。)

關鍵試航

1. 知道是一回事，執行 (practice) 又是一回事。

_____

2. 知道和執行是兩件不同的事。

_____

3. 了解不等同於實踐 (realization)。

_____

4. 女孩們坐在椅子上，面對著彼此。

_____

12　by oneself

The widow lived in that apartment **by herself**.

(那個寡婦獨自一人住在那棟公寓裡。)

用法說明

by oneself 表「靠自己；獨自地」，說明如下：

⑴表「靠自己」：(= without help = by one's efforts)

　　‧ She tried to solve the problem by herself. (她試著靠她自己解決問題。)

⑵表「獨自地」：(= alone)

　　‧ He walked in the dark lane by himself. (他獨自地走在暗巷裡。)

學習補給站

★ **for oneself**　為了自己 (= **for one's own sake**)

　　‧ I study hard for myself. (我為了我自己而努力讀書。)

★ **in itself**　本質上

　　‧ Money is not evil in itself. (金錢就本質而言不是邪惡的。)

★ **have something to oneself**　獨自享用，不與別人分享

　　‧ We'd better have an individual room to ourselves. (我們最好擁有各自的房間。)

關鍵試航

1. 自從妻子過世，他獨自一人住在大豪宅 (mansion) 中。

_____

2. 你可以靠自己負擔學費 (tuition) 嗎？

_____

3. 他為自己買了一輛車。

_____

4. 這隻狗自己開門。

_____

5. 野心的本質並不壞。

_____

13　that of...

The area of Taipei City is smaller than **that of** New York City.

(台北市的面積比紐約市的小。)

用法說明

1 在例句中 that of New York City = the area of New York City，為了避免重複出現在同一個句子中，所以用代名詞 that 代替 the area。請特別注意 that 之後一定要有片語加以限定，如本句為 of New York City。

2 如果所要代替的名詞為複數時，則以 those 代替之。以下例句以片語 in winter 來限定 those。

- The days in summer are longer than <u>those in winter</u>. (夏天的白天比冬天的白天長。)

學習補給站

★ **and that +** 副詞/副詞片語　而且

本片語經常接在完整子句後，以 that 代替該子句，其目的為避免重複並加強語氣。

- I used to make silly mistakes, <u>and that</u> very often.

(我以前會犯愚蠢的錯，而且經常如此。)

★ **that is (to say)** 　換句話說

　本片語為轉折詞，補充說明前面的完整子句，其他同義片語有：in other words 和 to put it differently。

・The fare is reduced for the elderly; <u>that is</u>, anyone above 65.

　　→ The fare is reduced for the elderly; <u>in other words</u>, anyone above 65.

　　→ The fare is reduced for the elderly; <u>to put it differently</u>, anyone above 65.

　　（年長者，即凡六十五歲以上者，票價有優待。）

關鍵試航

1. 北台灣的人口比南台灣的人口多。

_____

2. 二十世紀的汽車與現代的汽車相當不同。(those)

_____

3. 你必須交出答案卷，而且要馬上交。

_____

4. 端午節是農曆五月五日，也就是這個星期三。

_____

Exercises

I. Fill a proper word in each of the following blanks.

1. The widow lives in the little hut all _____ herself.

2. I did not put out the candle; it went out _____ itself.

3. Drinking is not bad _____ itself, but drinking too much can cause problems.

4. Jack is a selfish person; he does everything just _____ himself.

5. When it comes to choosing a boyfriend, a sense of responsibility is more important than _____ of humor to me.

6. The opinions given by the audience yesterday were totally the same as _____ of today.

II. Choose one proper answer.

_____ 1. The ears of a rabbit are longer than _____ .

    (A) a mouse   (B) those of a mouse

    (C) that of a mouse   (D) these of a mouse

_____ 2. My son did set the alarm for 5 o'clock; he woke up _____ .

    (A) in himself   (B) of himself   (C) by himself   (D) of his own

_____ 3. You must quit the job, and _____ immediately.

    (A) which   (B) it   (C) that   (D) those

_____ 4. I have two brothers; one is Alex, and the _____ is Andy.

    (A) one   (B) others   (C) other   (D) another

_____ 5. Some of the students speak English, and _____ speak Japanese.

    (A) another   (B) one   (C) the other   (D) the others

_____ 6. To make money is one thing; to spend it is _____ .

    (A) the other   (B) other   (C) another   (D) others

_____ 7. We lay on the lawn and looked at the sky, saying nothing to one _____ .

    (A) other   (B) another   (C) the other   (D) others

_____ 8. Her family died one after _____ .

    (A) another   (B) other   (C) the other   (D) others

_____ 9. We will accomplish the task you assigned in one way or _____ .

    (A) the others   (B) other   (C) some   (D) another

Unit 3　與助動詞有關的句型

14　used to V

My father **used to get up** early while at school.

(我爸爸在求學時期習慣早起。)

用法說明

1　used to 強調過去的習慣或狀態,常用來和現在作對比。used to 在此句型為助動詞,
後須接原形動詞。

・There <u>used to be</u> a graveyard near our school. (以前我們學校附近有一個墓園。)

2　be used to 則表示「從以前到現在一直都習慣做⋯」,to 在此為介系詞,後接名詞
或動名詞,試比較下列兩句:

・Tony <u>used to work</u> ten hours a day. (+ 原形動詞) (Tony 以前一天工作十小時。)

・Tony <u>is used to working</u> ten hours a day. (+ 動名詞) (Tony 習慣一天工作十小時。)

學習補給站

★ **be used to + <u>N/V-ing</u> = be accustomed to + <u>N/V-ing</u>**　習慣於⋯ (參考句型 **40**)

・I <u>am used to studying</u> until midnight every day.

→ I <u>am accustomed to studying</u> until midnight every day.

(我習慣每天讀書到深夜。)

・People living in Northern Europe <u>are used to the cold weather</u>.

→ People living in Northern Europe <u>are accustomed to the cold weather</u>.

(住在北歐的人習慣寒冷的天氣。)

關鍵試航

1.他們以前星期日都會上教堂。

2. 我讀大學時常常熬夜唸書。

_____

3. 我記得以前在轉角處有一家義大利餐廳。

_____

4. 我爸爸以前常常晨泳。

_____

5. 我爸爸一直都習慣晨泳。(used)

_____

15　had better + 原形 V

You **had better tell** the truth.

(你最好說實話。)

用法說明

1 had better 之後要接原形動詞；本句型常以縮寫形式 'd better 呈現。

- You'd better read as many books as you can when you are young.

  (你最好趁年輕時盡可能多讀書。)

2 had better 的否定句為：had better not...。

- We'd better not bother our grandfather. He is too sick to see us.

  (我們最好不要打擾爺爺。他病得太重所以不能見我們。)

3 另一個表「最好，不妨」的同義片語為：may as well...，否定句為 may as well not...。

- You may as well keep it secret.

  → You'd better keep it secret. (你最好將這件事保密。)

- We may as well not play jokes now.

  → We'd better not play jokes now. (我們現在最好不要開玩笑。)

學習補給站

★ **may/might as well A as B**　　與其 B 倒不如 A

本句型與 would rather A than B 意思相近，A 與 B 皆為原形動詞。(請參照 **70 would**

rather...than...)

- I <u>may as well</u> die <u>as</u> leave here.

  → I <u>would rather</u> die <u>than</u> leave here.

  (要我離開這裡我寧願死。→我寧願死也不願離開這裡。)

★ **may well + 原形 V = have good reason to V**　有足夠的理由…

may well 後接原形動詞，表達做某事的理由十分充分。

- You <u>may well get</u> mad at Tom, since he tried to deceive you.

  → You <u>have good reason to get</u> mad at Tom, since he tried to deceive you.

  (既然 Tom 試圖欺騙你，你大可對他發脾氣。)

關鍵試航

1. 此時你最好保持安靜。(had better)

_____

2. 我們最好不要取消此次會議。(had better)

_____

3. 為了健康的緣故，你不妨戒菸戒酒。(may as well)

_____

4. 要我去看一場無趣的電影，我寧願在家打盹兒。(might as well...as)

_____

5. 她有足夠的理由以她的獨子為榮。(may well)

_____

16　**may/might** have + V-en

Your girlfriend **may have returned** home by now.

(你的女友現在可能已經回家了。)

用法說明

1 對過去事物的推論

(1) **may have + V-en**　可能已經…

· Jack <u>may have heard</u> the news. (Jack 可能已經聽到消息了。)

(2) **might have + V-en** 當時可能… (但並未發生)

· Edward <u>might have got</u> lost but luckily he met my aunt.

(Edward 當時可能會迷路，幸好遇到了我阿姨。)

(3) **must have + V-en** 過去必定… (肯定的推測)

· He <u>must have told</u> you where he hid the letter. (他必定已經告訴你他把信藏在哪裡。)

(4) **cannot have + V-en** 過去不可能… (否定的推測)

· Mary <u>cannot have spoken</u> ill of us. (Mary 不可能說我們的壞話。)

2 對過去事物或狀態感到後悔

(1) **could have + V-en** 本來能夠… (過去能做而未做的事)

· I <u>could have finished</u> my homework, but I fell asleep.

(我本來可以做完功課，但我睡著了。)

(2) **should/ought to have + V-en** 早該… (過去該做而未做的事)

· You <u>should have listened</u> to me, but you didn't. (你早該聽我的，但你沒有。)

· We <u>ought to have left</u> the lab, but the teacher said no.

(我們早該離開實驗室，但老師說不可以。)

(3) **need not have + V-en** 當時不必…但卻… (過去不必做卻做了的事)

· You <u>need not have come</u> because that is not your business.

(你可以不必來，因為那不關你的事。)

關鍵試航

1. 我同學可能錯拿 (by mistake) 了我的傘。

_____

2. 他現在早該到達車站，但卻尚未現身 (turn up)。

_____

3. 你沒有必要這麼早來辦公室。

_____

4. 我本來可以順道接你，但是我突然覺得不舒服。

_____

17　would like to V

I would like to know why you have a green thumb.

(我想要知道你為什麼精通園藝。)

用法說明

1 would like to 的意思等於 want to，但 would like to 較禮貌。

- I would like to go with you.
  - → I want to go with you. (我想跟你一塊去。)

2 **Would you like...?**　客氣地詢問對方的需求

- Would you like (to have) another cup of coffee? (想要再一杯咖啡嗎？)

3 **would like + sb + to V**　禮貌地尋求他人的同意

- I would like you to come over immediately. (我希望你立刻過來。)

4 would like to 在口語中經常以縮寫 'd like to 的形式出現。

- We'd like to think about it for a while. (我們想要考慮一下。)

關鍵試航

1. 我想用航空 (airmail) 寄這個包裹。

_____

2. 我要一個三明治和一杯咖啡。

_____

3. 要不要再來一片蛋糕？

_____

4. 我希望你親自打電話給她。

_____

5. 我猜她想獨處一會兒。

_____

Exercises

I. Fill a proper word in each of the following blanks.

1. 你沒有必要把錢借給他。

   You _____ _____ _____ _____ him your money.

2. 他最好已經把工作做完了。

   He had _____ _____ done the job.

3. 你不妨把到歐洲旅行一事準備好。

   You _____ _____ _____ be prepared for your travel to Europe.

4. 一般人不習慣在公眾面前演說。

   People in general are not _____ _____ _____ a speech in public.

II. Choose one proper answer.

_____ 1. One _____ be careful when facing problems.

   (A) does not   (B) cannot   (C) should not   (D) had better

_____ 2. You'd better _____ up earlier tomorrow, or you'll be late.

   (A) get   (B) got   (C) getting   (D) be getting

_____ 3. You _____ well be proud of your son; he is good at almost everything in school.

   (A) ought   (B) can   (C) may   (D) must

_____ 4. We _____ rather not go with you if you insist on traveling by car.

   (A) could   (B) might   (C) should   (D) would

_____ 5. You cannot _____ Jacky this morning, because he left for America last night.

   (A) see   (B) have seen   (C) saw   (D) seen

_____ 6. You _____ as well go home now, or your parents will worry about you.

   (A) may   (B) ought   (C) should   (D) must

_____ 7. He _____ like to become an actor when he grows up.

   (A) will   (B) would   (C) should   (D) may

_____ 8. I _____ to him because he phoned me shortly afterwards.

   (A) needn't write   (B) needn't have written

   (C) needn't have wrote   (D) needn't had written

_____ 9. It _____ have rained very hard last night, for the ground is wet.

  (A) could   (B) should   (C) ought to   (D) must

_____ 10. This door ought to _____ a week ago.

  (A) have fixed (B) been fixed (C) fixed   (D) have been fixed

Note

Unit 4　與不定詞有關的句型

18　疑問詞 + to V

Read the instructions, and you'll know **what to do** next.

(閱讀說明書，你就知道下一步要做什麼。)

用法說明

1 疑問詞＋to V 形成名詞片語，在句中可作主詞、受詞或補語使用。代換為名詞子句時，須除去 to，並加入主詞及助動詞 should。

- <u>Where to go</u> is what I'm most concerned about. (主詞)

  → <u>Where we should go</u> is what I'm most concerned about.

  (我們該去哪裡才是我最關心的。)

- Tell me <u>how to get</u> along with a bossy person. (受詞)

  → Tell me <u>how I should get</u> along with a bossy person.

  (告訴我該如何和一個霸道的人相處。)

- The key to their success is <u>when to change</u> the traditional management system. (補語)

  → The key to their success is <u>when they should change</u> the traditional management system. (他們成功的關鍵在於該在什麼時候改變傳統的管理系統。)

2 how、where、when、why 為疑問副詞，形成不定詞片語時，若所接動詞為及物動詞，則後面要有受詞，若所接動詞為不及物動詞，則不須受詞。

- Frankly speaking, I don't know <u>how to ask</u> <u>my mom</u> for more allowance.

  (及物動詞 ask＋受詞 my mom) (坦白說，我不知道該如何要求我媽媽給我更多零用錢。)

- Jenny is still wondering <u>where to go</u> for her holiday. (不及物動詞 go)

  (Jenny 仍在考慮要去哪裡渡假。)

3 what、whom、which 為疑問代名詞，形成不定詞片語時，本身即為不定詞片語中的受詞，故其後不加受詞。

- Ashley asked her boyfriend <u>which to buy</u> for her father. (which 為 buy 的受詞)

  (Ashley 問她的男友該為她的父親買哪一個。)

· Nobody told Alex <u>whom to work with</u>, so he completed the job all alone.

(whom 為 with 的受詞)

→ Nobody told Alex <u>with whom to work</u>, so he completed the job all alone.

(沒有人告訴 Alex 該和誰一塊兒工作,所以他獨自一人完成了這份差事。)

4 whether 之後亦可加上不定詞,作「是否該…」解。

· I'm not sure <u>whether to forgive</u> him again or not. (我不確定是否該再一次原諒他。)

5 疑問詞 + N + to V,之中的疑問詞視同形容詞。

· All college freshmen must decide <u>which subjects to take</u> this semester.

→ All college freshmen must decide <u>which subjects they should take</u> this semester.

(大學新生們必須決定這學期修哪些科目。)

關鍵試航

1. 聽到這壞消息,他完全茫然 (at a loss) 不知該做什麼。

_____

2. 問題是如何和老闆解釋這次的會議不成功。

_____

3. 我媽媽不知道如何使用電腦。

_____

4. Louis 不知道該在會議中說什麼。

_____

5. Amy 不知道是否該信任一個有不良記錄的人。

_____

19 be to V

The ship **is to head** for Greenland this afternoon.

(這艘船今天下午即將前往格陵蘭島。)

用法說明

此句型可表示許多意義,比較下列用法:

(1)預定

- We <u>are to leave</u> by five.

 → We <u>are going to leave</u> by five. (我們預定五點前離開。)

(2)義務

- You <u>are to support</u> me because you are my best friend.

 → You <u>should support</u> me because you are my best friend.

 (你應該支持我，因為你是我最好的朋友。)

(3)可能

常見於被動語態，通常是否定句。

- Nobody <u>was to be found</u> in the deserted town.

 → Nobody <u>could be found</u> in the deserted town. (在廢棄的鎮上可能找不到任何人。)

(4)注定的命運

- The African slaves before liberation <u>were</u> never <u>to go</u> back to their hometown again.

 (解放前的非洲黑奴注定無法再回到他們的故鄉。)

(5)意圖

出現在 if 的子句中時，表示意圖。

- *If* we <u>are to enter</u> a good college, we should study harder.

 (如果我們想進入好的大學，就應更用功。)

關鍵試航

1. 游泳競賽預定在週末舉行。

_____

2. 你有義務在年底前將債務還清。

_____

3. 我想他的辦公室裡可能什麼線索也找不著。(Not a...)

_____

4. 由於過程中的粗心，這項實驗注定失敗。

_____

5. 如果你想要成功，就該盡你的全力。

_____

20 seem to have + V-en

Cathy **seems to have been** happy in her childhood.
(Cathy 的童年時期似乎過得很幸福。)

用法說明

1 seem to 之後使用完成式，表達「過去已經發生的事」。當 seem 為現在式時，是以目前的狀況推斷過去已發生的事；為過去式時，是以過去的狀況推斷已發生的事。注意其與 it seems that 的代換。(參考 **3 it seems that...**)

- She <u>seems</u> <u>to have been</u> happy then.
  - → It <u>seems</u> that she <u>was</u> happy then.

    (以她目前的狀況推斷) (現在看來，她當時似乎很快樂。)

- She <u>seemed</u> <u>to have been</u> happy then.
  - → It <u>seemed</u> that she <u>had been</u> happy then.

    (以她當時的狀況推斷) (她那時候似乎很快樂。)

2 hope、wish、want、expect 等動詞經常與 to have + V-en 連用，表示過去的希望、期待或欲求等心理的狀態。

- I <u>wished to have prepared</u> for the entrance exam. (真希望我早已將入學考試準備好了。)

關鍵試航

1. 從 John 的臉色 (complexion) 看來，他似乎是感冒了。

_____

2. 根據這張照片，Joy 年輕時似乎是個歌手。

_____

3. 媽媽告訴過我，祖母年輕時似乎是個美人。

_____

4. 他們似乎在那個晚宴 (dinner party) 上玩得很愉快。(It seems that)

_____

5. Tina 真希望在美國讀書時就已遇見 Daniel。

_____

21　感官/使役動詞 + O + 原形 V

The boss **made his workers work** seven days a week.
(那個老闆叫他的員工一星期工作七天。)

用法說明

1 感官動詞如 see、hear、feel、watch、listen to、notice 等，與使役動詞如 make、let、have 等，加了受詞後動作仍不完整，故須加原形動詞表達受詞所產生的動作。此原形動詞是由不定詞 to V 省略 to 而成。

- I <u>felt</u> the building <u>shake</u> when the train passed by. (當火車經過時，我覺得大樓在搖晃。)
- I <u>heard</u> my brother <u>sing</u> in the bathroom. (我聽到我弟弟在浴室裡唱歌。)
- Father <u>made</u> me <u>get</u> a cup of tea for him. (爸爸要我倒杯茶給他。)
- Mother <u>let</u> me <u>go</u> to the movies with my friends. (媽媽准許我和朋友們去看電影。)

2 以上句型若為被動語態，則不能省略 to。

- I *was made* <u>to clean</u> the toilet by my teacher. (我的老師叫我清掃馬桶。)

關鍵試航

1. 警察看到小偷跑走。

　　

2. 昨晚，Tom 聽見有人哭泣。

　　

3. 這學生的表現使老師感到很失望。

　　

4. Kelly 的媽媽准許她獨自去歐洲旅行。

　　

5. 這所學校的所有學生皆被要求每天背新字。

22 **cannot but** + 原形 **V**

Watching the news of the tsunami, Kitty **cannot but feel** sorry for the victims.

(看到有關海嘯的新聞，Kitty 不得不為罹難者感到難過。)

用法說明

注意 but 之後須接原形動詞。

· We <u>could not but respect</u> such a brave man. (我們不得不尊敬如此英勇的人。)

超級比一比

cannot but + 原形 **V**

= **cannot help but** + 原形 **V**

= **cannot help** + **V-ing** (help 之後須接動名詞)

· Hearing the melody, she <u>could not but shed</u> tears.

→ Hearing the melody, she <u>could not help but shed</u> tears.

→ Hearing the melody, she <u>could not help shedding</u> tears.

(聽到音樂的旋律，她不禁流下眼淚。)

學習補給站

注意下列兩個句型的 **but** 之後也接原形動詞。

★ **cannot choose but** + 原形 **V**　除了…別無選擇

· After the accident, the manager <u>could not choose but resign</u> from the post.

(那次意外之後，經理除了辭去職位別無選擇。)

★ **do nothing but** + 原形 **V**　只有…

· The residents <u>did nothing but complain</u> about the noise made by the factory.

(居民們對於工廠發出的噪音只知道抱怨。)

關鍵試航

1. 多數的觀光客都不禁讚嘆此美麗的風景。(cannot but)

2. 聽完 Tim 的笑話後，我不禁放聲大笑。(cannot help)

3. 當主持人 (host) 宣布 Stacy 是贏家時，她不禁哭了。(cannot help but)

4. 除了說實話，這罪犯別無選擇。

5. 那位老人只知道抱怨餐廳的服務不佳。

23　come to V

In time you will **come to realize** the importance of knowledge.

(最後你終將會了解知識的重要性。)

用法說明

1 此句型用於表達經過一段時間或經歷，某事終究會發生，意味著某種預期的結果逐漸產生，其後接原形動詞。

2 另外 get to V 也有類似的意思。get to 表示「逐漸…」。

- When you get to know him, you'll find he's very reserved.

  (你逐漸了解他之後，會發現他非常矜持。)

學習補給站

補充以下三個不定詞片語：

★ **prove to V**　證明是…

- Finally, the singer's scandal proved to be false.

  (最後這歌星的醜聞證明是虛構的。)

★ **turn out to V** 結果是…；原來是…

- What she said <u>turned out to be</u> false.

  (她所說的話原來是假的。)

★ **manage to V** 設法做到…

- I finally <u>managed to find</u> the solution to the tough problem.

  (我最後設法找到了這個棘手問題的解決之道。)

關鍵試航

1. 你最後怎麼和你女友熟識的？(come to)

_____

2. 你最後怎麼學會吹笛子 (flute) 的？(get to)

_____

3. 信不信由你，那個謠言將被證明是假的。

_____

4. 結果我們學校的籃球隊輸了這場比賽。

_____

5. 那名囚犯設法逃出了監獄。

_____

24 have something/nothing to do with...

I'm sure the actor **has something to do with** the scandal.

(我確信那位演員和那件醜聞有關係。)

用法說明

have 和 to do 之間加上 something (一些)、nothing (一點都沒有)、<u>much/a great deal</u> (很多)、little (幾乎沒有)、<u>a little/a bit</u> (少許) 等字時，可以表達出關係的程度。

- The boy said he <u>had</u> *nothing* <u>to do with</u> the bank robbery.

  → The boy said he didn't <u>have</u> *anything* <u>to do with</u> the bank robbery.

  (男孩說他和那起銀行搶案一點關係都沒有。)

- Human life has *much* to do with the air. (人類的生命與空氣有很大的關係。)
- Tom's success has *a little* to do with his mother. (Tom 的成功與他母親有些許關係。)
- The accident had *little* to do with me. (這件意外和我幾乎沒有關係。)

學習補給站

如果 have 與 to do 之間沒有任何修飾字時，則 **have to do with...** 可看成 have to 和 do with 兩個片語相加所組成，有「必須處理…」的意思。

- As a leader, you have to do with the problems.

(身為領袖，你必須處理這些問題。)

關鍵試航

1. 這場車禍和酒醉駕車有些關係。

_____

2. 財富與名聲和幸福幾乎沒有關係。

_____

3. 那場災難與天氣毫無關係。

_____

4. 大自然與動植物有很大的關係。

_____

5. 你必須處理這個問題，因為那是你的責任。

_____

25　be likely to V

Jerry is likely to abandon his original proposal.

(Jerry 有可能會放棄原來的提議。)

用法說明

be + Adj + to V，表達做某件事時的心態，為固定用法。如：

★ **be anxious to V = be eager to V**　渴望…的；急切希望…的

· We <u>were anxious to know</u> the truth. (我們急著知道實情。)

★ **be apt to V = be liable to V = be prone to V**　易於…；有…的傾向

· He <u>is apt to lose</u> his temper in difficult situations. (他在困境中易於發脾氣。)

★ **be ready to V**　準備好做…

· <u>Are</u> you <u>ready to go</u> now? (你準備好要走了嗎？)

★ **be sure to V**　務必…

· <u>Be sure to lock</u> the door before going out. (出去之前務必鎖上門。)

★ **be free to V**　做…是自由不受拘束的

· The journalists <u>are free to ask</u> any questions in this press conference.
(這場記者招待會中，記者可以自由發問。)

關鍵試航

1. 努力的人就有可能成功。

_____

2. 我們渴望聽到有關你的好消息。(anxious)

_____

3. 每當他生氣就容易對別人吼叫。(liable)

_____

4. 我已準備好搬至我的新家。

_____

5. 只要你努力 (stick to) 做你的研究，你一定會成功的。

_____

26　**have + the + 抽象名詞 + to V**

I didn't have the courage to tell the truth.

(我沒有勇氣說出真相。)

用法說明

1 have＋the＋抽象名詞＋to V，表「懷著某種心理狀態做某件事」。此為固定用法，功能類似副詞，修飾不定詞中的動作。如：

★ **have the kindness to V**　好意做…

· He has the kindness to answer my questions.

（他好意回答我的問題。）

★ **have the fortune to V**　很幸運能…

· She has the fortune to win the lottery.

（她很幸運能中樂透。）

★ **have the courage to V**　有勇氣做…

· No one in the class has the courage to challenge the teacher.

（班上沒有人有勇氣挑戰老師。）

★ **have the boldness to V**　有膽子做…

· Jenny has the boldness to turn down Jack's invitation.

（Jenny 很大膽地拒絕了 Jack 的邀請。）

★ **have the folly to V**　很愚蠢地去…

· You did have the folly to bribe the judge. (你去賄賂法官真是非常愚蠢。）

2 此等句型也可以用片語 so...as to V 或 ...enough to V 做代換。

· He has the boldness to climb up to the top of Mt. Jade alone.

→ He is so bold as to climb up to the top of Mt. Jade alone.

→ He is bold enough to climb up to the top of Mt. Jade alone.

（他真大膽，敢獨自爬上玉山山頂。）

關鍵試航

1. Adam 好意借給我他的摩托車。

_____

2. 她真幸運得到了頭獎。

_____

3. 那名男子大膽地躍入河中去救溺水的男孩。

_____

4. Iris 愚蠢到去相信 Jack 會娶她。(so...as to)

27 to tell the truth

To tell the truth, I have no interest in wealth and fame at all.

(說實話,我對名利一點興趣都沒有。)

用法說明

1 由不定詞所形成的片語可放於句首、句尾或句中,用來修飾主要子句,此類片語統稱為獨立不定詞片語,又稱為獨立副詞片語。如:

★ **to do someone justice**　替某人說句公道話

· To do him justice, Edwin is a bully-faced but kind-hearted guy.

(說句公道話,Edwin 是個面惡心善的傢伙。)

★ **to make a long story short = to be brief**　長話短說

★ **to begin with**　首先

★ **to sum up**　總而言之

· To sum up, you cannot choose but study hard.

(總而言之,除了努力唸書你別無選擇。)

★ **to make matters worse**　更糟的是

★ **to say nothing of**　更不用說

★ **to be frank**　坦白說

· To be frank, I would rather stay at home and watch TV.

(坦白講,我寧願待在家裡看電視。)

2 下列為幾個加上修飾性字眼後,所形成的獨立不定詞片語:

★ **strange to say**　說來奇怪

★ **needless to say**　自不待言;不用說

· The rich man is a typical miser. Needless to say, he views money as the most important thing in the world.

(這有錢人是典型的小氣鬼。不用說,他將錢視為世上最重要的東西。)

★ **not to mention**　　違論，更不用說；而且

· The toddler cannot walk steadily, <u>not to mention</u> running.

　(這個剛學步的小娃走路都走不穩，更別說跑步了。)

★ **not to speak of**　　更不用說

★ **so to speak**　　可以這麼說

關鍵試航

1.說實話，一開始我反對這個計劃。

_____

2.說來奇怪，這扇門自動開了。

_____

3.說句公道話，Jack 是我認識最誠實的人。

_____

4.坐在服務台前的那位老太太可以說是一本活字典。(..., so to speak, ...)

_____

5.更糟糕的是，我們才到達目的地就開始下雨。

_____

Exercises

I. Choose one proper answer.

_____ 1. If you are _____ your dream of being a flight attendant, you can receive some training.

(A) being realized (B) realized (C) to realize (D) to have realized

_____ 2. I _____ realize that Cindy is the only person who supports me in the office.

(A) become to (B) come to (C) like to (D) prove to

_____ 3. My father always makes me _____ the things that I don't want to do.

(A) done (B) doing (C) do (D) to do

_____ 4. Tom is shaking because he is _____ to talk with the teacher.

(A) anxiety (B) anxiously (C) to be anxious (D) anxious

_____ 5. After breaking up with her boyfriend, the girl did nothing but _____ all day.

(A) cry (B) to cry (C) crying (D) have been crying

_____ 6. We cannot do anything but _____ here for the president's coming.

(A) wait (B) to wait (C) waiting (D) to waiting

_____ 7. My mother had me _____ the dishes for her.

(A) doing (B) to do (C) done (D) do

_____ 8. Lawrence has nothing _____ with the car accident.

(A) to do (B) do (C) doing (D) done

_____ 9. Judy cannot but _____ her mother's order to go to college.

(A) obeying (B) obey (C) to obey (D) obeyed

II. Rearrange the words into a complete sentence.

1. 天空中什麼東西也看不到。(be, was, not, seen, to, a, thing)

_____ in the sky.

2. 老師叫我把這本書翻譯成英文。(translate, me, the book, had)

The teacher _____ into English.

3. 我們聽到他悲慘的消息只能嘆息。(hearing, when, but, sigh, couldn't)

We _____ his tragic news.

4. 做運動之前務必先暖身。(sure, to, be, warm)

Before taking exercise, _____ up first.

5. 我漸漸地體會到誠實的重要性。(to, come, the, importance, being, realize, honest, of)

I _____.

note

Unit 5　與分詞有關的句型

28　分詞構句⑴

Hearing the fire alarm, we all rushed out of the building.

(聽到火災警鈴聲，我們全都衝出大樓。)

用法說明

副詞子句演變而來的分詞構句視同副詞片語，修飾後面的主要子句，其中分詞構句中的動作用現在分詞 (V-ing) 時，表達出主要子句中主詞主動的行為，如例句中的 hear 是由 we 所產生的主動行為，可還原為 When we heard the fire alarm, we all rushed out of the building.。這類的分詞構句可傳達時間、理由、條件、讓步、附帶狀況等訊息，分別舉例如下：

⑴時間 (when, while, after, before...)

・ When she heard the joke, she burst out laughing.

　　→ Hearing the joke, she burst out laughing. (聽到笑話，她放聲大笑。)

⑵理由 (as, since, because...)

・ As I had nothing to say, I kept silent and left.

　　→ Having nothing to say, I kept silent and left.

　　　(因為我無話可說，所以保持沉默而離開。)

⑶條件 (if)

・ If you pay off the debt, you won't be sued.

　　→ Paying off the debt, you won't be sued. (如果你把債務還清，你就不會被告。)

⑷讓步 (although, though)

・ Although Daisy forgave Frank's wrongdoing, she didn't want to see him again.

　　→ Forgiving Frank's wrongdoing, Daisy didn't want to see him again.

　　　(雖然 Daisy 原諒了 Frank 做錯事，但是她不想再見到他。)

⑸附帶狀況 (and)

- Hank put on his glasses, and he began to read the novel.
  → Putting on his glasses, Hank began to read the novel.
  (戴上眼鏡，Hank 開始讀起小說。)

關鍵試航

1. 一到達機場，Karen 就打電話給她的父母。

_____

2. 因為沒事可做，她提早就寢。

_____

3. 向左轉，你就會看到捷運站。

_____

4. 雖然我了解你說的話，但是我並不同意。

_____

5. 揮著手，Joy 和她的父母說再見。

_____

29　分詞構句(2)

Scolded harshly by her teacher, Mary didn't shed tears.
(雖然被老師痛罵，Mary 沒有落淚。)

用法說明

1 完成式的分詞構句：Having + V-en，附帶傳達有關時間先後的訊息，用於從屬子句動作發生時間較主要子句為早時。

- After he <u>had finished</u> his science homework, he went out to play baseball.
  → <u>Having finished</u> his science homework, he went out to play baseball.
  (他完成科學作業之後，就出去打棒球了。)

2 被動語態的分詞構句：Being + V-en，或 Having been + V-en，其中過去分詞前的 being 和 having been 經常省略。

- <u>Since</u> these kids <u>are taken</u> good care of by parents, they will grow up happily.

→ (Being) taken good care of by parents, these kids will grow up happily.

(這些孩子們因為受父母好好地照顧而能快樂地成長。)

3 否定的分詞構句，無論表主動或被動，只要在分詞之前加上 not 或 never 即可。

・ Because the boy has never been to Disneyland, he is so excited about the trip next month.

→ Never been to Disneyland, the boy is so excited about the trip next month.

(因為那個小男孩從來沒去過迪士尼樂園，所以他對下個月的旅行感到很興奮。)

・ As he did not know what to do, he fiddled with his fingers.

→ Not knowing what to do, he fiddled with his fingers.

(因為不知如何是好，他撥弄著自己的手指頭。)

關鍵試航

1. 從遠處看去，那座山看起來像隻狗。

2. 做完功課之後，Gary 去游泳。

3. 與她的同事比較，Sherry 是個認真 (earnest) 的員工。

4. 我不知道該說什麼，所以會議上我保持沉默。

5. 沒有奪得旗子，奪標手 (catcher) 就掉到水中。

30 　frankly speaking

Frankly speaking, I do not appreciate the painting.

(坦白說，我並不欣賞這幅畫。)

用法說明

1 當分詞構句中的主詞與主要子句中的主詞不相同時，必須保留分詞構句中的主詞。

這種保有不同主詞的分詞構句稱為獨立分詞構句。

· If the weather permits, we can start off early.

→ Weather permitting, we can start off early. (如果天氣許可的話，我們可以早點出發。)

2 如果獨立分詞構句的主詞為一般所提到的 we、you、they 等人稱時，則省略之而形成固定用法，如：

★ **generally speaking**　一般來說

· Generally speaking, men are much stronger than women.

(一般來說，男人比女人強壯很多。)

★ **talking/speaking of...**　說到…

★ **considering...**　考慮到…

★ **taking...into consideration**　考慮到…

· Taking health into consideration, too much sugar and salt are harmful to us.

(考慮到健康，多糖多鹽對我們有害。)

★ **judging from...**　從…判斷

· Judging from his abilities, he is not suitable for the position.

(從他的能力考量，他不適合該職位。)

關鍵試航

1.從文法規則上來判斷，這個句子不正確。

_____

2.假期結束，勞工們立刻回到了他們的工作職位。

_____

3.如果我們考慮預算，該計劃就不可能被實行 (carry out)。

_____

4.說到打網球，Arthur 可說是無人能及。(Speaking)

_____

5.一般來說，男孩比女孩調皮。

_____

31　There be + S + 分詞

There are many **fans crowding** into the stadium.

(有很多的歌迷要擠進體育館。)

用法說明

當我們要表達某一個場所中有某個人物做了某一個動作，經常會使用 there is/are 的句型。本句型中真正的主詞放在 be 動詞之後，所以 be 動詞的單複數是由後面的真主詞來決定，動作則形成分詞的形式，現在分詞表示動作是主動的，過去分詞則表示動作是被動的。

⑴ **There be + S + V-ing**

・ There are a lot of bees flying around the garden.

　　→ A lot of bees are flying around the garden. (許多蜜蜂繞著花園飛。)

⑵ **There be + S + V-en**

・ There was only one coin left in the box.

　　→ Only one coin was left in the box. (盒子裡只剩下一枚硬幣。)

關鍵試航

1. 早上七點時很多人在等公車。

_____

2. 海上吹來一陣冷風。

_____

3. 他離開前只剩下一星期的假期。

_____

32　with + O + 分詞

My grandmother is sitting on the rocking chair **with her eyes closed**.

(我祖母正閉著眼睛坐在搖椅上。)

用法說明

1 在獨立分詞構句之前加上介系詞 with 就形成附帶條件的副詞片語。

· The man was standing on the corner *with* <u>his legs trembling</u>.

(那個人站在轉角處,雙腿打顫。)

· She was listening to me carefully *with* <u>her arms folded</u>. (她雙臂交叉,仔細聽我說話。)

2 以上的副詞片語演變的公式為:S + be + 分詞 → with + O + 分詞。

his legs *were* trembling → *with* his legs trembling

her arms *were* folded → *with* her arms folded

3 表附帶狀況的 with + O,其後的補語有下列三種:

⑴ **with + O + Adj**

· The girl stood there <u>with her face smiling</u>. (那個女孩面帶笑容站在那裡。)

⑵ **with + O + Adv**

· The lady was walking in the lobby <u>with her hat on</u>.

(那位女士戴著帽子走在大廳裡。)

⑶ **with + O + 介系詞片語**

· The detective stood in the dark lane <u>with a cigar in his mouth</u>.

(那個偵探站在暗巷中,口中叼著一根雪茄。)

關鍵試航

1. Vicky 眼睛閃閃發亮地對孩子們閱讀故事。

_____

2. 嘴裡都是食物時不要說話。

_____

3. 他戴著眼鏡看著兒子寄來的信。

_____

4. 她眼中含著淚水跟我說了個悲傷的故事。

_____

5. Leo 手裡拿著早餐衝入教室。

_____

33　have + O + V-en

Ivy **had her hair cut** in the beauty salon.

(Ivy 在美容院剪了頭髮。)

用法說明

1 have + O + V-en 有兩種意思：

　(1)使…

　　· I had my watch fixed by the repairman. (我把我的錶送去給維修人員修理。)

　(2)被…

　　· He had his digital camera stolen last night. (昨晚他的數位相機被偷了。)

2 判定受詞為主動或被動 (參考 **21** 感官/使役動詞 + O + 原形 V)

　(1)當 have 的受詞為動作的執行者，則句型為 **have + O + 原形 V/V-ing**。

　　· I had the porter carry my luggage into the truck.

　　　(我要求服務人員將我的行李拿到汽車車廂中。)

　　· We have the interviewee staying at the other room.

　　　(我們讓受訪者待在另一個房間裡。)

　(2)當 have 的受詞為動作的接受者，則句型為：**have + O + V-en**。

　　· She had the floor waxed. (她將地板打蠟。)

3 口語時常用 get 來取代 have，但若受詞為動作執行者時，動詞應用不定詞 (to V)。

　· The rich woman said she would get her servant to prepare breakfast for us.

　　(那有錢的女人說她會叫她的女傭為我們準備早餐。)

　· When did you get your watch fixed? (你何時把錶拿去修的？)

關鍵試航

1.我的錢包在擁擠的公車上被偷了。

_____

2.我想要修理洗衣機。(被動)

_____

3.這老人唯一的房子在火災中燒毀了。

_____

4. 我想要找人來清洗我的車子。(主動)

5. 書局明天前就會寄出你的書。(get)

34　make oneself understood

John tried hard to **make himself understood** in the meeting.

(John 在會議上努力設法讓別人理解他的意思。)

用法說明

在英文中，我們常見到 S + V + O + C 的句型，此種句型下的動詞雖然為及物動詞，但是由於加了受詞後意義仍不完整，故須加上補語，以補充說明受詞的狀態。此類動詞稱為不完全及物動詞，常見的有 see、watch、feel 等感官動詞或 make、have、get、keep 等使役動詞。

1 S + V + O + V-ing (受詞處於主動狀態)

- The careless mother left her baby crying alone in the cradle.

  (粗心的媽媽讓嬰兒獨自一人待在搖籃中哭泣。)

- I'm terribly sorry to have kept you waiting for hours.

  (我十分抱歉讓你等了好幾個鐘頭。)

2 S + V + O + V-en (受詞處於被動狀態)

- I saw the old man knocked down by the truck. (我看到那個老人被卡車撞倒。)

- I felt all the furniture moved by someone. (我覺得所有家具都被人移動過。)

關鍵試航

1. 你講英文別人能理解你的意思嗎？

2. 我爸爸昨天在車中小睡時，讓引擎開著。

3.現在我們有位訪客留在這兒與我們一起討論這個議題。

_____

4.因為噪音，所以我無法使別人聽到我說話。

_____

5.你最好先把你的電話修好。

_____

Exercises

I. Rearrange the words to make the sentence meaningful.

1. 有個人在樓下咖啡廳等你。(someone, is, for, you, waiting)

   There _____ in the café downstairs.

2. 他對他媽媽撒謊時心跳得很快。(heart, beating, with, his, fast)

   He told a lie to his mom _____.

3. 我一到家，我爸爸就要我去洗澡。(my father, me, had, taking)

   As soon as I arrived home, _____ a bath.

4. 公車司機發現有人遺留了一個錢包在車上。(a, left, there, was, purse)

   The bus driver found that _____ on the bus.

II. Choose one proper answer.

_____ 1. There are many foreigners _____ in Taipei.

   (A) live   (B) lived   (C) living   (D) lives

_____ 2. The girl smiled and ran to her father, with her eyes _____ brightly.

   (A) shine   (B) shining   (C) shined   (D) shone

_____ 3. After the concert, there is a lot of trash _____ on the ground.

   (A) throw   (B) throwing   (C) thrown   (D) threw

_____ 4. _____ ill, Fred still attended the meeting.

   (A) Be   (B) Being   (C) To be   (D) Been

_____ 5. I am sorry that I have kept you _____ so long.

   (A) wait   (B) waited   (C) to wait   (D) waiting

_____ 6. _____ his lost dog, the boy was very excited.

   (A) Finds   (B) Found   (C) Finding   (D) To find

_____ 7. Peter came into the classroom, _____ something on his shoulder.

   (A) carry   (B) carries   (C) carried   (D) carrying

_____ 8. The class _____ over, students went out of the classroom in a hurry.

   (A) being   (B) is   (C) be   (D) was

_____ 9. Strictly _____, the plan is not perfect.

   (A) speak   (B) spoke   (C) spoken   (D) speaking

_____ 10. _____ my parents' health, we avoid too much oil when cooking.

   (A) Considering   (B) Consider   (C) To consider   (D) Considered

Unit 6　與動名詞有關的句型

35　Upon/On + N/V-ing

Upon hearing the bad news, the helpless girl burst out crying.

(無助的女孩一聽到壞消息就放聲大哭。)

用法說明

1 upon/on + V-ing 強調某個時間點上所發生的事情，我們也可以用連接詞如 as soon as、the minute (that)、the moment (that)、the instant (that) 來替換。

- <u>On seeing</u> the clown, children felt excited.

  → <u>As soon as</u> *children saw* the clown, they felt excited. (小孩一看到小丑就感到興奮。)

- <u>On meeting</u> Alice, he decided to marry her.

  → <u>The moment (that)</u> *he met* Alice, he decided to marry her.

    (他一遇到 Alice 就決定要娶她。)

- <u>Upon leaving</u> her office, Jenny jumped into a cab.

  → <u>The instant (that)</u> *Jenny left* her office, she jumped into a cab.

    (Jenny 一離開辦公室就跳上一輛計程車。)

2 upon/on 之後也可以接名詞。

- <u>On arriving</u> at the hotel, the tourists hurried to relieve themselves.

  → <u>On their arrival</u> at the hotel, the tourists hurried to relieve themselves.

    (觀光客一到達旅館就匆忙去上廁所。)

學習補給站

★ **in + V-ing**　當…的時候

此句型中的 in 有 when 或 while 的意思。

- Take notice of your manners <u>in talking</u> to your teacher.

  → Take notice of your manners <u>when/while talking</u> to your teacher.

    (和老師說話時注意禮貌。)

關鍵試航

1. 祕書一發現事實就向雇主報告。(On + V-ing)

_____

2. 他一看到蜂窩拔腿就跑。(On + V-ing)

_____

3. 她大學一畢業就結婚了。(On + V-ing)

_____

4. 我一回到家就倒在床上。(On + N)

_____

5. 你穿越交通繁忙的街道時，務必小心。(in + V-ing)

_____

36 There is no + V-ing

There is no telling whether the event is true or not.

(無法分辨這個事件是真是假。)

用法說明

這個句型可以用以下數個句型代換：It is impossible to V，We cannot + 原形 V，Nobody can + 原形 V。

· There is no telling when he will resign from the post of manager.

→ It is impossible to tell when he will resign from the post of manager.

→ We cannot tell when he will resign from the post of manager.

→ Nobody can tell when he will resign from the post of manager.

(無法得知他何時會辭去經理的職位。)

學習補給站

★ **There is no use + V-ing** …是沒有用的 (參考 **1** 學習補給站)

· There is no use crying over spilt milk.

→ It is no use crying over spilt milk.

→ It is useless to cry over spilt milk. (【諺】覆水難收。)

★ **There is nothing like + <u>N/V-ing</u>**　沒有什麼是像…一樣

此句型中的 like 為介系詞，故其後接名詞或動名詞。本句型多用於形容某事很棒。

· <u>There is nothing like</u> a cold beer after a hot shower.

(沒有什麼是像在沖完熱水澡後來杯冰啤酒一樣好的。)

★ **How about + <u>N/V-ing</u>?**　…如何？

此句型表提議，亦可用 what about 替換，其後接名詞或動名詞皆可。

· <u>How about going</u> to the movies?

→ <u>What about going</u> to the movies? (你想去看電影嗎？)

關鍵試航

1. 要逃出陷阱是不可能的。

_____

2. 沒有人知道明天會發生什麼事情。

_____

3. 沒有什麼是像我媽做的牛肉麵一樣好的。

_____

4. 事後後悔已完成的事是沒有用的。

_____

5. 和這個固執的人爭執是沒有用的。

_____

37　Would/Do you mind + V-ing?

Would you mind lending me ten bucks?

(你介意借我十塊錢嗎？)

用法說明

1 mind 之後接動名詞作受詞，表示徵詢對方許可做該動作。

· <u>Would you mind opening</u> the window? (你介意開窗嗎？)

如要指出該動名詞所表示的動作或狀態屬於何人何物，可在動名詞前加上所有格。

· <u>Do you mind my sitting</u> here? (你介意我坐這兒嗎？)

2 如在非正式場合中要表示該動作或狀態屬於何人何物，則在動名詞前加上受格，此時動名詞為受詞補語，修飾其前面的受格。

- I don't mind him reading my book. (我不介意他看我的書。)

3 請注意此句型的回答句，因為 mind 本身就表示「介意」的意思，所以回答 yes 時表示「介意」，意即拒絕、不答應之意。如果要表示答應，則該用否定的形式回答。

- A: Would you mind me turning off the light? (你介意我關燈嗎？)
  B: Not at all. (一點也不介意。)
  No, I wouldn't. (我不介意。)
  Yes, I would. (對，我會介意。)

關鍵試航

1. 你介意幫我一個忙嗎？

_____

2. 這裡太擠了。請挪過去 (move over) 一些好嗎？

_____

3. 你介意我在此抽菸嗎？

_____

4.「你介意待會再打電話過來嗎？」「一點也不介意。」

_____

5. 你介意我參加你的生日宴會嗎？

_____

38　feel like + N/V-ing

I feel like taking a nap for a while.

(我想要小睡一會兒。)

用法說明

1 feel like 表「想要…」之意時，後可接動名詞或名詞。

- I don't feel like having a cup of tea.

→ I don't feel like a cup of tea. (我不想喝茶。)

2 feel like 表「摸起來像…」之意時，後須接名詞。

- The object feels like *wood*. (這物體摸起來像木頭。)

關鍵試航

1. 我想和他一塊兒隨音樂而舞。

_____

2. 今晚我不想散步。

_____

39　be in the habit of + V-ing

My father is in the habit of smoking after dinner.

(我爸爸習慣晚飯後抽菸。)

用法說明

1 be in the habit of + V-ing 為一般表示「習慣做…」的用法。另外，表達過去的習慣也可用 used to。

- They used to play basketball after school. (他們以前習慣在放學後打籃球。)

2 此句型可與 make it a rule to V 代換 (參考 **2** 學習補給站)

- My parents are in the habit of keeping early hours.
   → My parents make it a rule to keep early hours. (我父母習慣早睡早起。)

關鍵試航

1. 這位退休的將軍習慣在早晨慢跑。(habit)

_____

2. 我習慣於睡前洗澡。(rule)

_____

3. 我們以前經常談論未來。(used to)

_____

4. 我叔叔以前習慣在早上喝一杯咖啡。(used to)

40　be used/accustomed to + N/V-ing

He **is used/accustomed to dozing** off in class.

(他習慣在課堂上打瞌睡。)

用法說明

1 be accustomed to 與 be used to 的用法相同，其後都要接名詞或動名詞。

- You will be used to *the weather* here sooner or later.

  → You will be accustomed to *the weather* here sooner or later.

  (你遲早會習慣此地的天氣。)

2 類似的片語還有 get used to + V-ing 和 get accustomed to + V-ing，使用 get 時為強調動作的適應是漸進的。

- We got used to doing 50 push-ups every morning.

  (我們漸漸習慣每天早上做五十個伏地挺身。)

超級比一比

> I used to burn the midnight oil. (used to + 原形 V)
>
> (我以前常熬夜。)
>
> I am used to burning the midnight oil. (be used to + V-ing)
>
> (我習慣了熬夜。)

學習補給站

特別注意有些片語中的 **to** 為介系詞，故其後接名詞或動名詞。

★ **look forward to + N/V-ing**　期望；盼望

- I'm looking forward to receiving your letter soon. (我期望很快就收到你的來信。)

★ **stick to + N/V-ing**　　堅持

・Teachers should <u>stick to</u> <u>teaching</u> students to tell right from wrong.

(老師應堅持教導學生分辨對錯。)

★ **be dedicated to + N/V-ing**　　致力於…

・The professor <u>is dedicated to</u> <u>scientific research</u>. (這位教授致力於科學研究。)

★ **be opposed to + N/V-ing**　　反對

・Some residents <u>are opposed to</u> <u>building</u> car factories near their houses.

(有些居民反對在他們的住家附近興建汽車工廠。)

關鍵試航

1. 大部分的人不習慣白天睡覺。

_____

2. 你很快會習慣這種政治氣氛。

_____

3. 我漸漸習慣一個人在圖書館唸書。

_____

4. 她以前常常抱怨每一件事。

_____

5. 我們所有的人都盼望再見到你。

_____

41　prevent...from + V-ing

The heavy rain **prevented** us **from going** out.

(大雨阻止了我們外出。)

用法說明

表「阻止；阻擋」，與 stop...from + V-ing 意義相似。唯在 stop...from + V-ing 的用法中，from 可以省略。

・The rules <u>prevented</u> the accident <u>from happening</u>. (規範防止了意外的發生。)

· Her parents tried to stop her (from) studying abroad. (她的父母試圖阻止她出國讀書。)

學習補給站

以下補充兩個類似的用法：

★ **keep...from + V-ing**

· The preventative measures successfully kept the mad cow disease from spreading.

(預防性措施成功地阻止了狂牛症的蔓延。)

★ **hinder...from + V-ing**

· This unfortunate incident hindered him from marrying Linda.

(這個不幸事件阻礙了他與 Linda 的婚事。)

關鍵試航

1. 沒有人可以阻止我娶她。(prevent)

_____

2. 我的重感冒使我不能參加這次的會議。(prevent)

_____

3. Laura 的自尊心讓她沒有放聲大哭。(keep)

_____

4. 不要阻擋你的女兒實現夢想。(hinder)

_____

5. 你為何不阻止她惹上麻煩？(stop)

_____

42　When it comes to + N/V-ing

When it comes to playing basketball, he will give up everything, including his girlfriend.

(一談到打籃球，他會放棄一切，包括他的女友。)

用法說明

1 此句型後可接名詞或動名詞。

2 除了本章所提到的動名詞句型之外，以下再介紹用法類似的慣用句型。

★ **come near + V-ing**　幾乎；差一點

- The war came near taking place. (戰爭差一點就發生。)

★ **find/have difficulty (in) + V-ing**　對於…有困難

- He has difficulty (in) speaking English in public. (他對於公開說英文有困難。)

★ **be/keep busy (in) + V-ing**　忙於…

- My mother is busy (in) cooking in the kitchen now. (我媽正在廚房裡忙著燒飯。)

★ **What do you say to + V-ing?**　關於…你意下如何？

- What do you say to playing chess?
  → How about playing chess? (下棋好嗎？)

關鍵試航

1. 一談到彈鋼琴，Monica 在她班上不輸任何人。

_____

2. 小男孩差點被公車撞到。

_____

3. 他對於解決這個問題有困難。

_____

4. 學生們忙著準備期末考。

_____

5. 一塊兒吃晚飯好嗎？

_____

Exercises

I. *Fill a proper word in each of the following blanks.*

1. We could not go out because of the rain.

   → The rain kept us _____ _____ out.

2. As soon as my sister saw the cockroach, she began to scream.

   → _____ _____ the cockroach, my sister began to scream.

3. It is impossible to deny what you have said.

   → There is _____ _____ what you have said.

4. What do you say to seeing a movie tonight?

   → _____ _____ _____ a movie tonight?

II. *Choose one proper answer.*

_____ 1. Would you mind _____ the pepper to me, please?

    (A) to pass   (B) pass   (C) passing   (D) passed

_____ 2. We are looking forward _____ from you soon.

    (A) hearing   (B) hear   (C) to hear   (D) to hearing

_____ 3. Recently, Monica has been busy _____ for the final exam.

    (A) to prepare   (B) prepare   (C) to preparing   (D) preparing

_____ 4. The cook sticks _____ with natural ingredients.

    (A) to cook   (B) cooking   (C) cook   (D) to cooking

_____ 5. My parents are not accustomed _____ cold food for breakfast.

    (A) to eat   (B) eat   (C) eating   (D) to eating

_____ 6. It's no use _____ over spilt milk.

    (A) cry   (B) crying   (C) that you cry   (D) for you cry

_____ 7. We were used _____ out while we lived in L.A.

    (A) to eating   (B) eating   (C) to be eating   (D) eaten

_____ 8. The law prevents the river _____ being polluted.

    (A) toward   (B) to   (C) for   (D) from

_____ 9. When it comes _____ pictures, Tony is one of the best photographers in Taiwan.

    (A) to take   (B) take   (C) to taking   (D) taking

_____ 10. Listen to the music! I feel like _____ now.

    (A) to dance   (B) dancing   (C) to dancing   (D) dance

III. Read the translation and fill a proper word in each of the following blanks.

1. 一看到自己的名字在名單上，她便放心了。

   _____ _____ her name on the list, she felt relieved.

2. 在這麼冷的天氣裡，沒有什麼是像來杯熱巧克力一樣好的。

   There is _____ _____ a cup of hot chocolate in this cold weather.

3. 一說到旅遊，Ben 就變得很興奮。

   _____ _____ _____ _____ traveling, Ben becomes very excited.

Note

Unit 7　與關係詞有關的句型

43　what I am

I won't forget **what I am** when I achieve success.

(當我成功時，我不會忘了現在的自己。)

用法說明

1 what one is 表示「現在的自己」，相對地要表達「過去的自己」，可用 what one was
　或 what one used to be，都是特別強調一個人現在或過去的人格、樣貌、成就等。

　　· I'm grown up. I'm no longer <u>what I used to be</u>.

　　　→ I'm grown up. I'm no longer <u>what I was</u>. (我已經長大，不再是過去的我了。)

2 本句型的 be 動詞可以替換為其他的動詞如 has、does 等。

　　what one has　　(某人) 所擁有的…

　　what one does　　(某人) 的所作所為

　　· I don't care about <u>what he has</u> but <u>what he does</u>.

　　　(我在乎的不是他擁有什麼而是他的作為。)

關鍵試航

1.我之所以有今天都要歸功於我的父母。

_____

2.留學國外十年後，現在的 Tony 已非昔日的他了。(used to)

_____

3.一個人的幸福取決於個人的人格而非財富。

_____

4.他一夜之間花掉他所有的財產。

_____

65

44　what we call

The old man is **what we call** a walking dictionary.

(這位老人就是我們所謂的活字典。)

用法說明

1 本句型中的主詞可替換為 you、they、one 等代名詞，皆指一般人的看法，但須注意動詞單複數變化。
　　· The book is <u>what you call</u> a love story. (這本書就是所謂的愛情故事。)
2 若改為被動語態 what is called，意思仍相同。
　　· The book is <u>what is called</u> a love story.
3 另外有個同義片語，也有「所謂的」之意：so-called。特別注意其差異：so-called 為形容詞片語，修飾單數名詞時要置於冠詞 a(n) 或 the 之後。
　　· He is <u>what we call</u> a man of his word.
　　→ He is a <u>so-called</u> man of his word. (他就是所謂言而有信的人。)

關鍵試航

1. 我們的經理缺乏我們所謂的幽默感。

_____

2. 她先生就是人稱典型的英國紳士。(one)

_____

3. 我的房東就是你所謂的自私鬼。

_____

4. 他哥哥畢業於人稱最棒的大學。

_____

5. 我認為所謂的教育改革就是提升教育水準。(so-called)

_____

45　such...as...

James is not **such** a gentleman **as** you think.

(James 不是如你所想像的紳士。)

用法說明

1 在此句構中 such 用以修飾先行詞，而 as 視同關係代名詞，引導形容詞子句，以代替 such 所修飾的先行詞。

- You won <u>such</u> a good reputation <u>as</u> we expected. (你贏得了如我們所預期的好名聲。)

2 as 之後的形容詞子句中，若為 be 動詞則可省略。

- <u>Such</u> a diligent worker <u>as</u> *he (is)* will be promoted. (像他一樣勤勉的工人會被升遷。)

學習補給站

★ **such as...**　　　例如…

- I have been to many countries, such as Thailand, Korea, and Japan.

(我去過很多國家，像是泰國、韓國和日本。)

關鍵試航

1. 這本書正如我想的那麼簡單。(This book is such...as...)

2. 這件新聞正如之前媒體預測的是事實。(such a fact as)

3. Jack 喜愛做運動，像是打籃球和游泳。(such as)

46　no...but...

There is **no** one **but** loves his own country.

(沒有人不愛自己的國家。)

用法說明

1 關係代名詞 but 本身即是否定的意思,說明形容詞子句的否定,換言之,**but = that...not...** 。

- There is <u>no</u> one <u>but</u> loves his own country.

  → There is <u>no</u> one <u>that does not</u> love his own country. (每個人都愛自己的國家。)

2 再加上前面的 no 形成主要子句的否定,所以 no...but... 為雙重否定的句型,意即負負得正,因此例句可以翻譯為「每個人都愛自己的國家」。此句型的 no 也可替換為其他否定字,如 not、scarcely、hardly、never 等。

- There is <u>no</u> rule <u>but</u> has exceptions.

  → There is <u>no</u> rule <u>that does not</u> have exceptions.

  → Every rule has exceptions. (原則必有例外。)

關鍵試航

1.很少有人不愛自己的家庭。

_____

2.每個人都知道如何使用行動電話。

_____

3.幾乎沒有中國人不知道萬里長城。

_____

4.在我的故鄉,每次下雨必下大雨 (pour)。

_____

5.沒有一個學生不認識校長。

_____

47　All (that) + S + <u>have</u>/<u>has</u> to do is (to) V...

All we have to do is (to) try our best to carry out the project.

(我們所能做的一切就是盡全力實現計劃。)

用法說明

本句型的 all 為先行詞，其後的關係代名詞 that 通常被省略，be 動詞一定用單數形 (is 或 was)，主詞補語為省略 to 的原形不定詞。其中 all 可用 what 取代，此時的 what = the thing which，文法上稱為複合關係代名詞。

- <u>All</u> (*that*) you have to do now is (*to*) keep silent.

    → <u>What</u> you have to do now is (to) keep silent.

    → <u>The thing which</u> you have to do now is (to) keep silent.

    (你現在必須做的是保持沉默。)

學習補給站

★ **All + S + can do is (to) V...**　某人所能做的是…

- <u>All I can do is (to) pray</u> for you. (我所能做的是為你祈禱。)

★ **The best + S + can do is (to) V...**　某人所能做最好的一件事是…

- <u>The best I can do is (to) offer</u> you a proper job.

    (我最能做的就是提供你一份適當的工作。)

★ **All + S + V + is that...**　某人所…的一切是…

- <u>All you know is that</u> I am an ordinary businessman. (就你所知我是個平凡的生意人。)

關鍵試航

1. 現在 Alisa 所必須做的是努力讀書。

_____

2. 我們現在只能等待 Thomas 先生的到來。

_____

3. 現在你該做的是祝我幸運。

_____

4. 在那場比賽裡，我最多只能為你歡呼。

_____

5. 我所知道的是 Abel 與該竊案 (theft) 無關。

_____

48 This is why...

This is why he deserted his wife and kids.

(這就是他為什麼拋棄妻子和孩子的理由。)

用法說明

1 本句型的 this 也可以用 that 替換；why 為關係副詞，省略了其前面的先行詞 the reason。由 why 所引導的子句視同主詞補語，此句型前通常會有另一句子表達事件的「因」，而 why 之後的子句則表達事件的「果」。

· I didn't know Brian's phone number. That's why I didn't call him.

(我不知道 Brian 的電話號碼，那就是為什麼我沒有打電話給他的理由。)

2 意義同 This/That is the reason (that)...。

reason 之後的子句則為形容詞子句，補述 reason。

· This is the reason he has to resign immediately. (這就是他必須立即辭職的理由。)

學習補給站

★ **This/That is how...** 這就是…的方式

此句型中的 how 等於 the way that，表示「…的方式」，使用 the way 作先行詞時，關係代名詞 that 可以省略，故也等於 **This/That is the way (that)...**。

· This is how the ruler treats his people.

→ This is the way (that) the ruler treats his people.

(這就是這名統治者對待人民的方式。)

關鍵試航

1.這就是 Joe 為什麼還生我的氣的理由。(why)

_____

2.他不知道你的住址。那是他沒去拜訪你的理由。(why)

_____

3.這就是我們不能出席會議的理由。(reason)

4. 那就是你解決問題的方式嗎？

_____

5. 那就是 Jessie 和別人溝通的方式。(way)

_____

49　what + N

He lent me **what tools** he had.

(他把他所擁有的工具借給我。)

用法說明

1 本句型中的 what + N 為所謂的關係代名詞，此時的 what 則稱為關係形容詞，其意義等同於 all the...that...。

　・I imagine <u>what future</u> I can hope for in my life.

　　→ I imagine <u>all the future that</u> I can hope for in my life.

　　　(我想像我在人生中所能期盼的未來。)

2 表示極少的時候亦可在 what 的後面加上 little 或 few，不可數名詞用 little，可數名詞用 few。

　・The girl won't give up <u>what *few* opportunities</u> she has for being a dancer.

　　(這女孩不會放棄她現有成為舞者的極小機會。)

關鍵試航

1. 他把所有的錢都給了太太。

_____

2. 我把所能省下的時間花在社會現象的研究。

_____

3. Buck 向他老闆說了他心中所有的想法。

_____

4. 我願意為你做任何微小的服務。

_____

50   ..., who/whom/which...

He has two sons, **who** practice medicine in the U.S.

(他有兩個兒子，兩人都在美國執業。)

用法說明

1 例句中的關係代名詞 who 之前有逗點時，who 所引導的關係子句是一種非限定用法，即補述用法。

2 在一般限定的關係子句中，關係代名詞若作為受詞，可以省略。但須注意，若關係子句為補述用法而不是限定用法時，關係代名詞就算作為受詞也絕對不能省略。試比較下列兩句：

Dr. Li, whom I am going to invite, is respected by all his students.

(李博士受到他所有學生的尊敬，他將受到我的邀請。)

(補述李博士這人將受到我邀請，為補述用法，whom 不可省略。)

That man (whom) I am going to invite is respected by all his students.

(將受到我邀請的那個人受到他所有學生的尊敬。)

(限定我要邀請的人是受到學生尊敬的，為限定用法，whom 可以省略。)

3 非限定用法的 which，可以取代前面子句中的一部分或全部的概念。

· I like *my school*, which is famous for its strict discipline.

(which 指的是學校) (我喜歡我的學校，它以紀律嚴格而聞名。)

· Some students *don't study hard*, which will make them fail the exam.

(指「不用功」這件事) (有些學生不用功，不用功會造成考試失敗。)

· *People pursue wealth and fame*, which tends to cause stress.

(指「追求名利」這件事) (人們追求名與利，這樣容易造成壓力。)

4 當關係代名詞之後有 S + think、S + feel、S + know 等插入語時，注意其後動詞的單複數仍以先行詞為判斷依據。

· June was deserted by *the man* who she thought *was* her Mr. Right.

(June 被原以為是如意郎君的人所拋棄。)

關鍵試航

1. Alina 有兩個女兒，兩個都主修法律。

　　_____

2. 這是台北 101，它是由一位國際知名的建築師所設計。

　　_____

3. 有些人不吃早餐，這樣有害健康。

　　_____

4. 國王被他認為忠心的手下背叛。

　　_____

5. 她是我認識適合這個任務的最佳人選。

　　_____

Exercises

I. Fill a proper word in each of the following blanks.

1. 這是計劃進行的方式。

   This is _____ _____ the project goes.

2. 每位觀眾都為他的演說所感動。

   There was _____ audience _____ was _____ by his speech.

3. 要選擇對你有益的朋友。

   Choose _____ friends _____ will be beneficial to you.

4. 人們唯有了解自我才會有自信。

   Men can only _____ confident by understanding _____ they are.

II. Choose one proper answer.

_____ 1. I like to visit my teacher, _____ lives in Tainan.

   (A) who　　　　(B) whom　　　　(C) that　　　　(D) she

_____ 2. I like Tom Cruise, _____ is really a handsome actor.

   (A) who　　　　(B) whom　　　　(C) which　　　　(D) whose

_____ 3. Please lend me _____ money you have now.

   (A) who　　　　(B) what　　　　(C) which　　　　(D) that

_____ 4. Edward is not such a man _____ would tell a lie.

   (A) that　　　　(B) as　　　　(C) who　　　　(D) but

_____ 5. There is no one _____ hates death and poverty.

   (A) that　　　　(B) as　　　　(C) who　　　　(D) but

_____ 6. There is no one _____ does not love his parents and siblings.

   (A) that　　　　(B) but　　　　(C) as　　　　(D) which

_____ 7. It is education that makes us _____ we are.

   (A) what　　　　(B) when　　　　(C) where　　　　(D) why

_____ 8. That is _____ everybody here hates the boss so much.

   (A) what　　　　(B) how　　　　(C) why　　　　(D) who

Unit 8　與時間有關的句型

51　no sooner...than...

The patient had **no sooner** seen a pool of blood **than** she fainted.

(病人一看到那灘血就昏倒了。)

用法說明

1 此句型牽涉兩個過去動作的相對時間關係，含 no sooner 的主要子句動作較早發生，故用過去完成式：had + V-en，than 引導的從屬子句動作較晚發生，則用過去式。本句型可與 as soon as 的句型代換，但 as soon as 所連接的主要或從屬子句都用過去式。

　　・We *had* no sooner *arrived* at the station than the train *left*.

　　　→ As soon as we *arrived* at the station, the train *left*. (我們一到達車站火車就離開了。)

2 no sooner 為否定副詞，若置於句首時，主要子句要形成倒裝句。

　　・No sooner *had I come back home* than I turned on the TV. (我一回到家就打開電視機。)

3 另外一個句型：hardly/scarcely...when/before... 與 no sooner...than... 同義，均表「一…就…」之意。

　　・No sooner had the thief seen the police than he ran away.

　　　→ As soon as the thief saw the police, he ran away.

　　　→ Hardly had the thief seen the police when he ran away.

　　　→ Scarcely had the thief seen the police before he ran away.

　　　(小偷一見到警察拔腿就跑。)

關鍵試航

1.媽媽一聽到這個壞消息就臉色蒼白。(no sooner)

_____

2.我一離開家就下雨了。(As soon as)

_____

3. 弟弟一回到家沒有洗澡就睡了。(No sooner)

4. 小女孩一見到吠叫的狗就放聲大哭。(Hardly)

5. 老師一下課，學生就衝出教室。(Scarcely)

52 not...long before...

I had **not** waited **long before** she showed up.

(我等了不久她就出現了。)

用法說明

1 此句型所要表達的是某個事件發生之前的時間並不久。當此句型用於敘述過去的事時，主要子句用過去完成式，before 所引導的子句用過去式。若要用此句型表示一段確定的時間，也可將句中的 long 替換為較確定的時間。

- They had <u>not</u> worked with each other *half a month* <u>before</u> they began to complain.

  (他們在一塊兒工作不到半個月，就開始抱怨。)

2 注意常見於文章中的句型是：It <u>is</u>/<u>was</u> not long before... 或是未來式：It will not be long before...。

- <u>It was not long before</u> I saw him. (不久之後我就見到他。)
- <u>It will not be long before</u> the police officer appears. (不久那名警員將會出現。)

關鍵試航

1. Joannie 從大學畢業後不久，就找到工作了。

2. 我們沒等很久火車就來了。

3. 他們結婚不到一個月就開始爭吵。

4. 不久該謠言就證實是假的。

_____

5. 不久之後，這公司將開始宣傳它的新型電腦。

_____

53 not...till/until...

I did**n't** go to bed **until** two o'clock last night.

(昨晚我直到兩點才睡。)

用法說明

1 本句型雖然有 not 出現，但是中文不以否定意思翻譯，而是從 until 開始，再接到前面的主要子句，也就是「直到…才…」。

- Kenny did**n't** show up at the party <u>until</u> it was close to an end.

  (Kenny 直到派對要結束了才出現。)

2 本句型常將 not until 放在句首，形成倒裝句，用以強調「直到某個時候」。

- <u>Not until</u> yesterday *did I know* I passed my English test.

  → I did <u>not</u> know I passed my English test <u>until</u> yesterday.

    (直到昨天，我才知道我的英文測驗通過了。)

3 本句型也經常和強調句 It is...that... 相結合，形成 It is not until...that... 的句型，但是注意與說明 2 不同之處在於此用法不必倒裝。

- <u>It was not until</u> yesterday <u>that</u> I knew I passed my English test.

關鍵試航

1. 直到失去健康，我們才知道健康的價值。(not...until)

_____

2. 直到回到家，我才發現我丟了傘。(Not until)

_____

3. 直到 Tom 告訴了她，她才知道她男友在美國的情況。(It was not until)

_____

4.直到火車消失在 Judy 的視線，她才離開月台。(not...until)

54　It is...since...

It is about three years **since** I last came here.

(上次我來此地已經約三年了。)

用法說明

1 本句型因出現 since 子句，故主要子句也可以完成式替換：It has been...since...。

2 也可把期間置於句首，表示一段時間已經過去了，句型為：...has/have passed since...。
since 之後一定是過去時間，所以動詞恆為過去式；而主要子句的動詞單複數需視時間主詞的單複數而定。

- It has been three years since we entered this senior high school.
  - → Three years have passed since we entered this senior high school.
    (自從我們進入這所高中已經三年了。)

3 注意此句型的替換如下：

- It is five years since he studied abroad.
  - → It has been five years since he studied abroad.
  - → Five years have passed since he studied abroad.
  - → He has studied abroad for five years. (他出國讀書已經五年了。)

關鍵試航

1.這家超市已經成立六年多了。(It has been...since)

2.我祖父生病已經兩年了。(Two years)

55　every time...

Every time my uncle pays me a visit, he brings me a big surprise.
(每次我叔叔來拜訪我,都帶給我大驚喜。)

用法說明

1 本句型 every time 為連接詞的用法,用以連接從屬及主要子句。

- Every time I feel sleepy, I drink a cup of coffee. (每當我想睡覺,我就喝杯咖啡。)

2 every time 可以替換為 each time 或者 whenever,意思皆相同。

- Every time I pass by the train station, I recall my childhood.
  - → Each time I pass by the train station, I recall my childhood.
  - → Whenever I pass by the train station, I recall my childhood.

    (每當我經過火車站,我就想起我的童年。)

學習補給站

以下三個片語都是與時間有關的連接詞,其後都接子句。

★ **(the) next time...**　下一次

- (The) Next time you come to Taipei, I will take you around.

  (下一次你來台北,我會帶你四處逛逛。)

★ **(the) last time...**　最後一次;上一次

- Jill looked young and confident (the) last time I met her in Paris.

  (我最後一次在巴黎遇到 Jill 時,她看起來年輕而有自信。)

★ **by the time...**　到了…的時候

- The house will have been decorated by the time you come back from your honeymoon. (你度蜜月歸來時,屋子就裝潢好了。)

關鍵試航

1. 每次祖母來時,她都會帶禮物給我。

2. 每當我們下棋時，我的爸爸都會贏。

---

3. 下次我們見面時，Tom 會把我要的文件帶給我。

---

4. 我上一次看到 Pablo 時，他才五歲。

---

5. 我希望我們到達目的地時就不再下雨。

Exercises

I. Fill a proper word in each of the following blanks.

1. Smith didn't go abroad until he graduated from college.

→ It was _____ _____ Smith graduated from college _____ he went abroad.

2. It is three years since Ally left her hometown and worked in the city.

→ It _____ _____ three years since Ally left her hometown and worked in the city.

II. Choose one proper answer.

_____ 1. It was not long _____ a helicopter arrived on the scene to rescue the survivors of the plane crash.

(A) when　　(B) after　　(C) while　　(D) before

_____ 2. They didn't give up the plan _____ they realized they had no time to carry it out.

(A) before　　(B) after　　(C) until　　(D) since

_____ 3. Five years _____ passed _____ she worked in Taipei.

(A) have; since　(B) has; when　(C) have; for　(D) has; after

_____ 4. The tower will have been completed _____ you get your master's degree next year.

(A) every time　(B) last time　(C) next time　(D) by the time

_____ 5. No sooner _____ recovered from a heart attack _____ he made a speech on TV to thank those who had helped him.

(A) he had; since　　　　　(B) had he; than

(C) he have; before　　　　(D) have he; whenever

_____ 6. It was not long _____ the party started.

(A) when　　(B) after　　(C) before　　(D) if

Note

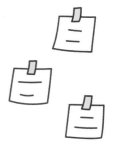

Unit 9　與假設或條件有關的句型

56　If...should...

If the suspect **should** not confess his crime, what will you do?

(萬一嫌犯不認罪,你該怎麼辦?)

用法說明

1 此句型用以表示未來不太可能發生或實現機率很小的假設,意思是「萬一…」。if 子句中助動詞用 should,而主要子句使用現在式助動詞 will、can、may 時,表示未來發生的可能性較高;使用過去式助動詞 would、could、might 時,表示未來發生的可能性較低。

2 若主要子句為命令句,則主要子句中的 that 子句應用現在式助動詞 <u>will/can/may</u> + 原形 V。

・ If anyone <u>should</u> come to my office, *tell* him or her that I <u>will</u> show up in the afternoon. (萬一有任何人來我辦公室,告訴他或她我下午會出現。)

學習補給站

★ If + S + were to + 原形 V..., S + 過去式助動詞 (**should/would/could/might**) + 原形 V...　如果…

此句型用來表達未來絕不可能發生的假設。

・ If the earth <u>were to</u> stop rotating, he <u>would give away</u> his property.

(如果地球停止旋轉,他就會捐出他的財產。)

關鍵試航

1.萬一發生大地震,我們該怎麼辦?

2.萬一有任何人打電話給 Peter,就說他明天會回來。

3. 萬　我上學又遲到，我願意接受老師的處罰。

4. 如果你能加入我們這一隊，我們就會是冠軍了。(were to)

5. 如果太陽從西邊升起，Maggie 就會改變心意嫁給你。(were to)

57　If it were not for..., ...

If it were not for your timely help, I would fail again.

(要不是你及時的幫助，我就會再次失敗。)

用法說明

1 此句型若用以表與現在事實相反的假設，if 子句中的 be 動詞恆用 were，不可用 was，主要子句則用過去式助動詞 would、could、should、might。

- If it were not for the rain, crops could not grow. (若非有雨水，農作物無法生長。)

2 若是表示與過去事實相反的假設，if 子句動詞用過去完成式：had + V-en，主要子句為：過去式助動詞 (would/should/could/might) + have + V-en。

- If it had not been for Kevin's blood donation, the patient would have been dead.

  (若非當時有 Kevin 捐的血，病人早就死了。)

3 用法說明 1 與 2 的兩個句型亦可省略 if 之後，將 were 或 had 置於句首形成倒裝句。

- If it were not for hard work, you couldn't win the game.

  → Were it not for hard work, you couldn't win the game.

    (要不是努力，你不可能贏得比賽。)

- If it had not been for the scholarship, I wouldn't have gained the master's degree.

  → Had it not been for the scholarship, I wouldn't have gained the master's degree.

    (要不是有那份獎學金，我不會得到碩士學位。)

關鍵試航

1. 如果沒有空氣，我們就無法生存。

_____

2. 若非老闆的忠告，我的計劃不會成功。

_____

3. 兩年前若非教授的支持，我們可能早已放棄計劃。

_____

4. 若非有音樂，這個世界必定單調。(Were)

_____

5. 昨天要不是你父母在場，我就會懲罰你。(Had)

_____

58　without/but for...

Without TV, life might be boring. → **But for** TV, life might be boring.

(如果沒有電視，生活可能很無趣。)

用法說明

1 without... 和 but for... 的句型可以表示與現在事實相反、與過去事實相反的兩種假設語氣，其區別在於主要子句中的動詞型態，如果是 would/should/could/might + 原形 V，則表示與現在事實相反；如果是 would/should/could/might + have + V-en，則表示與過去事實相反。其意思與句型 **57** 完全相同，也可以互相替換。

- Without the crack, I *would buy* the vase immediately.

  → But for the crack, I *would buy* the vase immediately.

  → If it were not for the crack, I *would buy* the vase immediately.

  → Were it not for the crack, I *would buy* the vase immediately.

  (要不是這個花瓶有個裂縫，我會立刻買下它。)

- Without the negotiation, the trade *could not have been settled* down.

  → But for the negotiation, the trade *could not have been settled* down.

  → If it had not been for the negotiation, the trade *could not have been settled* down.

› Had it not been for the negotiation, the trade *could not have been settled* down.

(如果當時沒有協商談判，交易就無法完成。)

2 若 with 置於句首，亦有假設的意思。

· With your devotion, our program could go smoothly.

→ If we had your devotion, our program could go smoothly.

(有你的犧牲奉獻，我們的計劃才有可能順利進行。)

關鍵試航

1. 要不是有風，今天就會是個舒適的好天。(Without)

_____

2. 要不是下雨，我們就可以去野餐。(But for)

_____

3. 要不是有暴風雨，我們早已經抵達目的地。(But for)

_____

4. 有你的支持，我才可能會成功。(With)

_____

5. 有了電話，你可以輕鬆地和世界各地的朋友連絡。(With)

_____

59 If only...

If only I could fly freely like a bird.

(要是我能像鳥自由地飛就好了。)

用法說明

本句型像 I wish... 一樣都是表達某種願望。當表達與現在或未來事實相反的願望時，用過去式動詞；當表達與過去事實相反的願望時，動詞則用過去完成式。

· If only you could accompany me all the time.

→ I wish you could accompany me all the time. (但願你能一直陪伴我。)

學習補給站

以下四個句型都為假設法句型的應用，表達某種願望的語氣。關於假設法的時態運用請參見此句型的用法說明。

★ **Would (that)...** 　要是…有多好

- Would that I could see him before he drew the last breath.

  (要是我能在他嚥下最後一口氣前見他一面有多好。)

★ **Would to God that...** 　願上帝…有多好

- Would to God that I would win the lottery. (願上帝讓我中樂透該有多好。)

★ **How I wish...** 　真希望…

- How I wish the world had no war. (我真希望世上無戰爭。)

★ **Oh, that...** 　真希望…

- Oh, that there were no crime in society. (真希望社會上沒有犯罪。)

關鍵試航

1. 要是我能彈鋼琴彈得和貝多芬一樣該有多好。

————————————————————————————

2. 但願飛機早已準時降落。

————————————————————————————

3. 願上帝讓我再年輕一次。

————————————————————————————

4. 我真希望擁有一輛自己的汽車。(How)

————————————————————————————

5. 要是我能環遊世界該有多好。(Oh, that)

————————————————————————————

60　**It is time** + 假設法過去式

It is time you **went** to bed.

(你該就寢了。)

用法說明

1 It is time 後面必須接過去式子句，表示與現在事實相反的假設語氣，實際上該動作尚未做，而且希望對方能去做。

- It is time (*that*) he hit the sack. (該是他上床睡覺的時候了。)

2 在 time 之前加上 high 或 about 用以強調時間點，但整個句法不變。

- It is *high* time you went to school. (你該去學校了。)
- It is *about* time she did the cooking. (該是她去做飯的時候了。)

3 如果子句中要加上助動詞，則用 should + 原形 V。

- It is time we left for the train station.
  → It is time we should leave for the train station. (我們該前往火車站了。)

4 也可以代換為下列句型：

- It is time Mary faced the music.
  → It is time for Mary to face the music. (該是 Mary 面對事實的時候了。)

關鍵試航

1. 我們該離開了。

_____

2. 你該完成寒假的作業了。

_____

3. 你該去上班了。(high)

_____

4. 我們該為考試做準備了。(about)

_____

5. 你們該交答案卷了。

61 Suppose/Supposing (that) ...

Suppose (that) the economy collapsed, what would the country be?

(假如經濟崩潰，這個國家會怎麼樣？)

用法說明

suppose 或 supposing 的用法與 if 雷同，其後的 that 可以省略，視為連接詞，引導子句表達有可能的假設，或與事實相反的假設。

- Supposing (that) you have one billion dollars now, what will you do with it?
  (假設說你現在有十億，你會怎麼處理這筆錢？)

學習補給站

以下二個句型與 suppose/supposing 在表達未來可能性的假設時用法雷同，表示一種對未來的預測，其後所接子句的動詞或助動詞要用現在式。

★ **on condition (that)...**　假如⋯

- We will start to practice the first step of our proposal on condition (that) there is no opposition. (假如沒人反對，我們就可以開始進行提案的第一步。)

★ **in case...**　萬一⋯

- In case I oversleep, please wait for me for a while. (萬一我睡過頭，請等我一下。)

關鍵試航

1. 要是你是老闆，這次的事件你會怎麼處理？(Suppose)

_____

2. 如果你遲到，你會有什麼樣的藉口？(Supposing)

_____

3. 假設你考試不及格，你會怎麼和你父母解釋？(Suppose)

_____

4. 只要晚上十點之前回到家，你要去哪都可以。(on condition that)

_____

5. 萬一下雨，籃球賽就會取消。(In case)

_____

62 as/so long as...

As long as you have confidence in our cooperation, we'll make it.
(只要你對我們的合作有信心，我們就會成功。)

用法說明

1 如 as long as 所連接的子句表達「…的時候」，可用 while 替換；如表達「…的條件」，則可用 if only... 或 provided/providing that... 替換。

- I won't be afraid <u>as long as</u> you are here.
  → I won't be afraid <u>while</u> you are here. (只要有你在，我就不害怕。)
- You may go to the movies <u>as long as</u> you finish your homework.
  → You may go to the movies <u>if only</u> you finish your homework.
  (只要你功課做完就可以去看電影。)

2 若 <u>as/so</u> long as 所連接的子句為副詞子句，必須以現在式代替未來式。

- <u>As long as</u> *you pay off the debt*, you can go abroad. (只要你債務還清就可以出國。)

學習補給站

以下二個句型與上述的句型形似，但與假設法無關，通常出現在句首，形成副詞子句，修飾其後的主要子句。

★ <u>as/so</u> far as...　就…所…

- As far as we know, there is still no life form being found on Mars.
  (就我們所知，火星上仍沒發現任何生物。)

★ <u>as/so</u> far as...be concerned　就…而言

- As far as traffic safety <u>is concerned</u>, the design of this bridge is not good.
  (就交通安全而言，這條橋的設計沒有很好。)

關鍵試航

1.只要我有空，我一定會寫信給你。

2.只要你參加會議，就可以得到一份禮物。

_____

3.只要你同意為我設計房子，我不介意你索取多少錢。

_____

4.就我所知，Tim 是個守信用的人。

_____

5.就我而言，沒有什麼比健康重要。

_____

63　命令句 + and/or...

Stand still, or I'll shoot.

(站著不要動，否則我會開槍。)

用法說明

1 此句型中的 and/or 子句表達由命令句所得出的推論或結果。命令句 + and... 可以代換為 if...；而命令句 + or... 可以代換為 if...not... 或 unless...。

- Follow the school regulations, and you won't be punished.

  → If you follow the school regulations, you won't be punished.

  (遵守校規，你就不會被懲罰。)

- Park your car at the parking lot, or you will be fined.

  → If you don't park your car at the parking lot, you will be fined.

  → Unless you park your car at the parking lot, you will be fined.

  (把車停在停車場，否則你會被開罰單。)

2 本句型中的 or 可以用 or else 或 otherwise 替換，注意 or else 是連接詞，otherwise 是副詞，所以替換時注意標點符號的使用。

- Eat more, or you will not have enough energy for mountain climbing.

  → Eat more, or else you will not have enough energy for mountain climbing.

  (多吃一點，否則你會沒有足夠的體力爬山。)

- Talk to your family, or they won't understand your feelings.

  → Talk to your family. Otherwise, they won't understand your feelings.

(和家人談一談，否則他們不了解你的感受。)

3 有時句意明確時會將動詞省略，而命令句改以名詞的形式出現。

- <u>Do</u> ten more push-ups, and I'll let you leave.
  - → <u>If you do</u> ten more push-ups, I'll let you leave.
  - → <u>Ten more push-ups</u>, and I'll let you leave.

  (再做十個伏地挺身，我就讓你離開。)

關鍵試航

1. 努力就會成功。(and)

_____

2. 快一點兒，否則你上學會遲到。(or)

_____

3. 睡一會兒，不然你明天會很累。(or else)

_____

4. 馬上完成這份工作，否則你會喪失升遷的機會。(Otherwise)

_____

5. 再多一分努力，你一定會達成目標。(One more)

_____

Exercises

I. Fill a proper word in each of the following blanks.

　1. I'm quite sure I will succeed. But what could I do if I _____ fail?

　2. _____ _____ his poor health, he would be a successful businessman.

　3. If the sun _____ to rise in the west, our friendship would change.

　4. If it _____ not _____ your advice, I would be at a loss what to do.

II. Choose one proper answer.

_____ 1. If Mr. Bain _____ in a day or two, I would wait for him.

　　(A) will return　　(B) has returned　　(C) were to return　　(D) had returned

_____ 2. If Carol _____ late, give her the message I left.

　　(A) were coming　　(B) would come　　(C) should come　　(D) were come

_____ 3. _____ you to die, I would take care of your children.

　　(A) Had　　　　(B) Only　　　　(C) Were　　　　(D) If

_____ 4. Had you told her the truth, she _____ such a silly mistake.

　　(A) might not make　　　　　　(B) would not make

　　(C) have not made　　　　　　(D) might not have made

_____ 5. _____ for his help, I could not reach the goal.

　　(A) But　　　　(B) Without　　　(C) Not　　　　(D) Unless

_____ 6. If he _____ not that poor, he would study abroad.

　　(A) would　　　(B) is　　　　　(C) were　　　　(D) had been

_____ 7. _____ that he were here to help all of us.

　　(A) Could　　　(B) Should　　　(C) Would　　　(D) Had

_____ 8. Oh, if only I _____ that beautiful dress when I was a child.

　　(A) have　　　(B) had　　　　(C) should have　　(D) had had

Note

Unit 10　與比較有關的句型

64　as + Adj/Adv + as + N/子句...

You should read **as much as** he does.

(你應該和他一樣多閱讀。)

用法說明

1 我們可以用 as...as... 表示兩種人事物是一樣的。
- Johnny is <u>as</u> *patient* <u>as</u> his mother. (Johnny 和他媽媽一樣有耐心。)
- My dog is *not* <u>as/so</u> *hairy* <u>as</u> yours. (我的狗不像你的狗那麼多毛。)

  (否定用法 not so...as... 可與 **66 not so much A as B** 做比較)

2 若要表示程度，則在 as...as... 之間加上程度形容詞，如 many、much 等。注意，在選擇程度形容詞時，應考量是用來修飾可數或不可數名詞，如 many 接可數名詞，much 接不可數名詞。
- You should take <u>as</u> *much exercise* <u>as</u> I do. (你應該和我一樣多運動。)
- Bob couldn't eat <u>as</u> *many hamburgers* <u>as</u> Joe could in a short time.

  (Bob 無法和 Joe 一樣在短時間內吃那麼多個漢堡。)

關鍵試航

1. 我和我父親一樣固執 (stubborn)。

_____

2. Frank 不像他弟弟一樣去過那麼多國家。

_____

65　...times as...as

What I need is **three times as** much money **as** you can lend me.

(我所需要的錢是你能借我的三倍。)

用法說明

1 在比較級中使用倍數時，要注意倍數需放在 as 之前。三倍以上用 three/four/five...times，兩倍用 twice，一半用 half，四分之一用 quarter。

- I have <u>twice</u> <u>as</u> many books <u>as</u> you do. (我擁有的書是你的兩倍。)
- We used <u>half</u> <u>as</u> much gas <u>as</u> we expected. (我們用了預期中一半的汽油。)

2 分數亦可運用在此句型中，表示「幾分之幾的…(量)」。注意分數的表示法：先說分子，再說分母；分子用基數，分母用序數；當分子大於 1 時，分母加 s，形成複數型。例：1/3 → one-third

$\qquad$ 2/3 → two-third*s*

$\qquad$ 3/4 → three-fourth*s*

- The price of the diamond has risen by <u>one-third</u> <u>as</u> high <u>as</u> it was.

(這顆鑽石的價錢已經比以前提高了三分之一。)

3 表達倍數關係時亦可將 as...as 替換為 than 的用法：...times + 比較級 + than...。

- The house is <u>three times</u> <u>as</u> expensive <u>as</u> mine.
- → The house is <u>three times</u> <u>more</u> expensive <u>than</u> mine.

(這棟房子比我的房子貴三倍。)

4 將所有格放在倍數之後：...times the + N + of + 所有格的受格，或 ...times + 所有格 + N。其中名詞會根據文意而選用 size (面積)、age (年紀)、price (價格)、length (長度)、width (寬度)、height (高度) 等字。

- The house is <u>three times</u> <u>the size of mine</u>. (面積) (這棟房子面積是我家的三倍大。)
- Tom's mother is <u>twice</u> <u>his age</u>. (年紀) (Tom 的媽媽年紀比他大兩倍。)
- Eddie's car is <u>half</u> <u>the price of ours</u>. (價格) (Eddie 的車價錢是我們車的一半。)

關鍵試航

1. 房價 (the housing prices) 比十年前上漲 (rise) 了兩倍。

_____

2. 他答應提高我現有薪水的四分之一。

_____

3. 這部吉普車比那部汽車貴三倍。(than)

_____

4.體育館是教室的十倍大。

_____

5.這個游泳池是那個游泳池的二分之一長。

_____

66　not so much A as B

He is **not so much** a general **as** a soldier.

(與其說他是將軍不如說他是個小兵。)

用法說明

1 本句型意味著是後者而非前者，即是 B 而不是 A。可與其他句型代換：B rather than A 或 more B than A。

- She is <u>not so much</u> an amateur actress <u>as</u> a drama writer.

  → She is a drama writer <u>rather than</u> an amateur actress.

  → She is <u>rather</u> a drama writer <u>than</u> an amateur actress.

  → She is <u>more</u> a drama writer <u>than</u> an amateur actress.

  → She is <u>less</u> an amateur actress <u>than</u> a drama writer.

  (與其說她是業餘的演員，不如說她是戲劇作家。)

2 A 和 B 除了是名詞之外，也可以是動詞、形容詞或其他片語，重點是 A、B 必須為對等的詞性。

- The little girl was <u>not so much</u> *hurt* <u>as</u> *frightened*.

  → The little girl was <u>less</u> *hurt* <u>than</u> *frightened*.

  (與其說小女孩受傷了，不如說她受驚嚇了。)

- The policy does <u>not so much</u> *damage* the original system <u>as</u> *change* it.

  → The policy *changes* the original system <u>rather than</u> *damage* it.

  (與其說這個政策損害了原始制度，不如說是改變了它。)

學習補給站

★ **not so much as... = not even...**　甚至不⋯

此句型中的 so much as 僅有副詞的功能，用以強調 not 之意，故其後接原形動詞。

- Her husband did <u>not so much as</u> <u>remember</u> their wedding anniversary.

  (她先生甚至不記得他們的結婚週年紀念日。)

★ **without so much as + V-ing**　甚至沒有…

此句型中的 so much as 仍舊是副詞的作用，故 without 後須接動名詞。

- He took my bicycle away <u>without so much as</u> <u>saying</u> a word.

  (他甚至一個字都沒說就拿走我的腳踏車。)

關鍵試航

1. 與其說我媽媽是妻子不如說是家裡的女傭。

   _____

2. 我躺下，與其說是在睡覺不如說是在沉思。

   _____

3. 你說的話不如你做的事重要。

   _____

4. 這個病人甚至無法記得自己的住址。

   _____

5. Kevin 甚至沒有通知家人就出國了。

   _____

67　the same...as...

I have **the same** laptop **as** you do.

(我有一台和你相同的筆記型電腦。)

用法說明

1 在此句構中的 as 視同關係代名詞，代替 the same 所修飾的先行詞，表示同類或同樣的人或事物。

- I have <u>the same</u> trouble <u>as</u> you are faced with. (我和你面對一樣的煩惱。)

2 如果將 as 改為 that，則中譯的「像…一樣」就改為「就是…」，表示同一人或事物。

· This is <u>the same car</u> <u>that</u> he picked me up yesterday. (這就是他昨天載我的那一輛車。)

關鍵試航

1. 這支手錶和我在巴黎買的一樣。

_____

2. 這就是 Cindy 拿給我看的那支錶。

_____

3. 你又犯了和上次一樣的錯誤。

_____

4. Annie 和 Ben 是同一天出生的。

_____

68　A as well as B

He is a surgeon **as well as** a novelist.

(他是外科醫生也是小說家。)

用法說明

1 as well as 也可以連接兩個主詞，A as well as B，重點在於強調前者，所以動詞的單複數以 A 決定。

· <u>Lucy</u> as well as I <u>is</u> Mr. Wang's student. (Lucy 和我一樣是王先生的學生。)

2 as well as 是對等連接詞，所以前後所接的詞性一定要相同。

· Mary ever lived _in Germany_ <u>as well as</u> _in America_. (Mary 曾住過德國和美國。)

3 本句型可代換為 not only B but also A 或 not merely B but A as well。

· Tony works hard in the nighttime <u>as well as</u> in the daytime.

→ Tony works hard <u>not only</u> in the daytime <u>but also</u> in the nighttime.

→ Tony works hard <u>not merely</u> in the daytime <u>but</u> in the nighttime <u>as well</u>.

(Tony 不僅白天工作努力，晚上也很努力。)

學習補給站

以下兩個句型有比較級的形式，但是沒有比較之意。

★ **as early as...** 早在…

- As early as the 17th century, the wheel has been invented.

  (早在十七世紀時，輪子就被發明了。)

★ **as good as...** 幾乎等於是…

- He as good as turned us down. (他幾乎等於是拒絕了我們。)

關鍵試航

1. 他是位流行歌手，也是位老師。

_____

2. 我和 Jeri 一樣都錯了。

_____

3. 他的主意無論在理論上或實際面上都很完美。

_____

4. 早在十四世紀羅馬就是座很大的城市。

_____

5. 這場火災後，這家公司幾乎等於毀了。

_____

69 the + 比較級..., the + 比較級...

The older Mary grows, the more beautiful she becomes.

(Mary 年紀愈大，變得愈漂亮。)

用法說明

1 本句型是由兩個句子合併而成，例如：

I have many. (我有很多。) → I have more. (我有更多。)

I want many. (我要很多。) → I want more. (我要更多。)

找出形容詞或副詞，將其改為比較級。然後將比較級移到句首，並且在前面加上定冠詞 the，將兩句合併：

- The more I have, the more I want. (我擁有愈多，就想要更多。)

2 也可代換為 as＋S＋V＋比較級，S＋V＋比較級。

- The more preparations you make, the fewer troubles you will get into.

  → As you make more preparations, you will get into fewer troubles.

  (你準備的愈充分，碰上的麻煩愈少。)

3 此種句型中的動詞為 be 動詞時，可以省略。若主詞及動詞為 it is，亦一併省略。

- The sooner (it is), the better (it is). (愈快愈好。)
- The more haste, the less speed. (【諺】欲速則不達。)

學習補給站

★ **(all) the ＋ 比較級 ＋ for/because...**　　因為…而更加…

本句型中的 all the ＋ 比較級，主要是作副詞用，放在動詞之後修飾動作。for 之後接名詞，because 之後接子句，都是表達理由。

- He studied all the harder for failure.

  → He studied all the harder because he had failed. (因為失敗他更加努力讀書。)

★ **none the ＋ 比較級 ＋ for/because...**　　不會因…而更…

本句型中的 none the ＋ 比較級，也是作副詞用，放在動詞之後修飾動作。for 之後接名詞，because 之後接子句，都是表達理由。

- She is none the more pessimistic for her poverty.

  → She is none the more pessimistic because she is poor. (她不會因貧窮而悲觀。)

關鍵試航

1. 一個人愈貪心損失會愈多。

_____

2. 我們爬得愈高看得愈遠。

_____

3. 天氣愈冷我們的生活愈困難。

_____

4. 正因為她有缺點我更加愛她。

5. 雖然他很富有卻不快樂。

70 would rather...than...

The soldier **would rather** die **than** surrender.

(士兵寧願死也不投降。)

用法說明

1 would rather 和 than 之後都要接原形動詞，強調前面的動作比後者重要。

2 有時不特別強調後者的動作時，than 及其後的動作皆可一併省略。

- I would rather go to the movies on the weekend (than go during the week).

  (我寧可週末去看電影，也不要平日去。)

3 本句型的否定形式為：**would rather not...**。

- I would rather not eat anything. (我寧可什麼都不吃。)

4 與 would sooner...than.../would as soon...as... 代換

- I would rather be punished than cheat you.

  → I would sooner be punished than cheat you.

  → I would as soon be punished as cheat you.

  (我寧願被處罰也不願欺騙你。)

關鍵試航

1. 這種天氣下，我寧可待在家裡也不願出去。

2. 她寧可獨自一個人去美國旅行。

3. 他寧可不要搭飛機去歐洲。

4. Ken 寧願餓肚子也不願吃他姊姊煮的菜。(sooner)

_____

5. 他寧願立刻辭職也不道歉。(as soon)

_____

71　much more...

He can play tennis well, **much more** badminton.

(他的網球打得好,遑論羽球。)

用法說明

1 much more... 用於肯定句,否定句則改為 much less...。

- She _cannot_ tell a lie, <u>much less</u> commit a crime. (她不會說謊,更不用說犯罪。)

2 much <u>more/less</u> 視同對等連接詞,之後除了名詞、動詞之外,也可以接片語,但重要的是前後詞性必須一致。

- Parents are responsible _for children's food and clothing_, <u>much more</u> _for their safety_.

  (父母要負責子女的衣食,更遑論其安全。)

3 另外幾個同義的獨立不定詞片語有:not to speak of...、not to mention...、to say nothing of...,可用於肯定句或否定句,後接名詞或動名詞為其受詞。

- He cannot speak Spanish, <u>not to speak of</u> _writing_ it.

  → He cannot speak Spanish, <u>not to mention</u> _writing_ it.

  → He cannot speak Spanish, <u>to say nothing of</u> _writing_ it.

  (他不會說西班牙文,更不用說寫西班牙文了。)

4 let alone 亦是同義片語,可用在肯定句及否定句中,視同連接詞。

- A newborn baby cannot walk, <u>let alone</u> _run_. (新生嬰兒不會走路,遑論跑步。)

關鍵試航

1. 我祖父會讀日文,更不用說講日文。(much)

_____

2. 我祖母不會說中文，更不用說寫中文。(much)

_____

3. 我媽媽喜歡寫音樂，更不用說是聽音樂。(not to mention)

_____

4. 我弟弟不敢踩蟑螂，更不用說是殺人了。(not to speak of)

_____

5. Tom 一點也不尊敬他的父母，更不用說是感謝他們了。(let alone)

_____

72 what's more

She is intelligent; **what's more**, she is kind and friendly.

（她聰明；此外，她善良且友善。）

用法說明

1 what's more = moreover = furthermore 表「此外」之意，在段落中作轉折詞用。

- He lost his wallet; <u>what's more</u>, he forgot to bring his key.

  （他的皮夾掉了，此外，他還忘了帶鑰匙。）

2 若將 more 改為 better：what's better 表「更好的是」。

- The house is big; <u>what's better</u>, it is close to the supermarket.

  （這房子很大，更棒的是，它靠近超級市場。）

3 若將 more 改為 worse：what's worse 表「更糟的是」。

- I was late for school today; <u>what's worse</u>, I forgot to bring my homework.

  （我今天上學遲到，更糟的是，我忘記帶作業。）

另一個片語：what makes matter worse 亦可表「更糟的是」。

- The approaching typhoon is huge; <u>what makes matter worse</u>, the island was just stricken by an earthquake.

  （逼近的颱風很巨大，更糟的是，此島才剛被地震侵襲。）

關鍵試航

1. Jill 的母親很漂亮；此外，她還非常高雅。

_____

2. 今早我很晚起床；更糟的是，我今天有五科的考試。

_____

73　know better than to V

I know better than to trust a crook like him.

(我不會笨到去相信像他一樣的無賴。)

用法說明

1 本句型 to 之後接原形動詞，表示「夠明事理而不至於去做該動作」。本句型可做以下的代換：

- He <u>knows better than</u> <u>to beat</u> her.
  - → He <u>is not so foolish as</u> <u>to beat</u> her.
  - → He <u>is not such a fool as</u> <u>to beat</u> her.
  - → He is <u>so wise that</u> he <u>won't</u> beat her. (他不至於笨到去打她。)

2 know better 本身有「能清楚分辨」之意。

- I <u>know better</u> than you do. (我比你更清楚。)

學習補給站

★ **think better of...**　深思後作罷

此句表示在深刻思考後，因覺得不適當而決定放棄該想法。

- Eric though of studying abroad, but he <u>thought better of</u> it.

  (Eric 本想出國留學，但深思後作罷。)

★ **more than one can help**　愛莫能助

表示超過一個人能力範圍所能做的事。

- Never brag <u>more than you can help</u>. (別吹噓一些你幫不上忙的事。)

關鍵試航

1. 我們不會笨到希望敵人仁慈。

   _____

2. 員工不會笨到和老闆爭吵。

   _____

3. 你這個年齡應該能清楚明辨了。

   _____

4. Adam 本來同意了我們的要求，但深思後作罷。

   _____

5. 別花費超過你能力範圍的金額。

   _____

74　no more...than...

Peter is **no more** intelligent **than** his brother (is).

(Peter 和弟弟一樣不聰明。)

用法說明

1 本句型的重點在於強調 no more 否定的部分，than 為對等連接詞。

   · _A bird_ is <u>no more</u> a mammal <u>than</u> _a frog_ is. (鳥和青蛙一樣不是哺乳類動物。)

2 代換為 not...any more than...。

   · She can <u>no more</u> dance <u>than</u> you can.

     → She can<u>not</u> dance <u>any more than</u> you can.

     → She can<u>not</u> dance, <u>nor</u> can you. (她和你一樣不會跳舞。)

學習補給站

注意比較以下十分類似的句型，所謂差之毫釐失之千里，務必辨識清楚：

★ **not more...than...**　沒有比⋯更⋯

   · Kent is <u>not more</u> outstanding <u>than</u> his brother (is).

     (Kent 沒有比他哥哥傑出。)

關鍵試航

1. 河馬和驢子一樣不是馬。(no more)

___

2. 我和你一樣不會打網球。(any more)

___

3. 他沒有比你更仔細。

___

75　no less than...

No less than 200 students came down with the flu this month.
(這個月多達二百名學生感染流行性感冒。)

用法說明

1 no less 會產生負負得正的效果，也就是表示肯定之意，與 as many as 或 as much as 同義。

- I have to pay <u>no less than</u> two thousand dollars to the landlord every month.
  → I have to pay <u>as much as</u> two thousand dollars to the landlord every month.
  (我每個月要付給房東多達兩千元整。)

2 注意以下易混淆的片語及其代換：

no less than... = as <u>many/much</u> as　多達

no more than... = only　只有

not less than... = at least　至少

not more than... = at most　至多

- The boy has <u>no less than</u> $100.
  → The boy has <u>as much as</u> $100. (這男孩有多達一百元的錢。)
- The boy has <u>no more than</u> $100.
  → The boy has <u>only</u> $100. (這男孩只有一百元。)
- The boy has <u>not less than</u> $100.
  → The boy has <u>at least</u> $100. (這男孩至少有一百元。)

- The boy has <u>not more than</u> $100.

  → The boy has <u>at most</u> $100. (這男孩最多只有一百元。)

關鍵試航

1. 多達一千人在這場地震中喪生。(less)

_____

2. 王先生每年所賺的薪水多達五百萬。(less)

_____

3. 從我家走到學校只需五分鐘。(more)

_____

4. 我們至少要在機場待上三小時。(less)

_____

5. 你最多再等我半小時。(more)

_____

76 Nothing is so...as...

Nothing is so important as health.

(健康是最重要的。)

用法說明

1 否定詞＋be 動詞＋so＋原級＋as... 表示最終的結果是「最⋯」，雖然句子使用原級，但表達的卻是最高級。

- <u>No other</u> student in my class <u>is so</u> _lazy_ <u>as</u> John.

  → John is _the laziest_ student in my class. (John 是我班上最懶惰的學生。)

2 除了本句型外，以下三種情形皆可表示最高級之意：

(1) the＋最高級

(2)否定詞＋be 動詞＋比較級＋than...

(3)比較級＋than any other＋單數名詞...

- Money is the most important to him.

    → Nothing is so important as money to him.

    → Nothing is more important than money to him.

    → Money is more important than any other thing to him. (對他而言金錢最重要。)

關鍵試航

1. 對我而言時間最重要。(nothing is so...as)

   _____

2. Shirley 是全校最漂亮的女孩。(more...than any other)

   _____

3. 超速駕車是最危險的。(the most)

   _____

4. 台北是台灣最大的都市。(No other...so...as)

   _____

77　be superior to...

Joyce's analytical ability **is superior to** Mike's.

(Joyce 的分析能力優於 Mike。)

用法說明

superior、inferior、junior 和 senior 等字為形容詞，本身即可作比較級用，比較時，須加上 to，才可接比較的人或事物。

- Teddy's design is inferior to Peggy's.

    → Teddy's design is worse than Peggy's. (Teddy 的設計比 Peggy 的差。)

- Henry is senior to Lesley by two years.

    → Henry is older than Lesley by two years. (Henry 比 Lesley 年長兩歲。)

關鍵試航

1. 新來的同事比我們年長。(senior)

   _____

2. 我的英文能力比我的弟弟差。(inferior)

   _____

3. Kathy 比我小一歲。(junior)

   _____

4. Carol 相機的品質比 Jennifer 的好。(superior)

   _____

Exercises

I. Fill a proper word in each of the following blanks.

1. The man is a salesman rather than a factory worker.

   → The man is _____ so _____ a factory worker as a salesman.

2. My grandpa gave me as much as 2,000 dollars last New Year.

   → My grandpa gave me _____ _____ than 2,000 dollars last New Year.

3. I like Taipei best of all the cities in Taiwan.

   → I like Taipei better _____ _____ _____ _____ in Taiwan.

4. Emily is quite as charming as her elder sister.

   → Emily is _____ _____ charming than her elder sister.

II. Rearrange the word order to make the following sentences complete.

1. 我和 Jack 一樣不會拉小提琴。(play the violin, can no more, Jack, than, can)

   I _____ .

2. 這家餐廳的服務優於那家的。(is, to, the service, superior, of)

   The service of this restaurant _____ that one.

III. Choose one proper answer.

_____ 1. Peter decided to help us, but later he thought _____ of it.

   (A) better　　　(B) more good　　(C) the better　　(D) the best

_____ 2. David Smith is not so _____ as you are.

   (A) strong　　　(B) stronger　　　(C) strongest　　(D) the strong

_____ 3. New York City is larger than _____ city in the U.S.

   (A) any　　　　(B) all　　　　　(C) any other　　(D) all the

_____ 4. The cloth you have is _____ that.

   (A) superior than　(B) better to　　(C) worse than　　(D) inferior than

_____ 5. Joan would rather _____ the dishes than clean the table.

   (A) doing　　　(B) did　　　　　(C) do　　　　　(D) done

_____ 6. No other house is so expensive _____ John's.

   (A) than　　　　(B) as　　　　　(C) to　　　　　(D) so

_____ 7. Linda doesn't like dessert, _____ chocolate cake.

    (A) much less   (B) no more   (C) what's more   (D) less than

_____ 8. The older we are, _____ .

    (A) and the more money we want   (B) we will be happy

    (C) the wiser we may be   (D) the richest you are

_____ 9. Larry is _____ his brother.

    (A) as three times heavy   (B) three times as heavy

    (C) as three times as   (D) three times as heavy as

_____ 10. Mr. Peterson has as _____ jobs as Mr. Davidson.

    (A) more   (B) heavy   (C) much   (D) many

Unit 11　與否定有關的句型

78　not always...

My job is interesting, but **not always** easy.

(我的工作很有趣，但未必容易。)

用法說明

1 本句型表達部分否定，意味著不全然如此。英文中有些副詞或代名詞，如：all、always、necessarily、both、exactly、entirely、wholly、altogether、quite、every、absolutely 等，一旦加上否定字詞，則形成部分否定。

2 區分部分否定與全體否定：

- My boss doesn't always eat lunch. (部分否定) (我老闆未必都吃中飯。)
  My boss never eats lunch. (全體否定) (我老闆從不吃中飯。)

- Not every person likes pizza. (部分否定) (並非每個人都喜歡披薩。)
  Nobody likes pizza. (全體否定) (沒有人喜歡披薩。)

- Not all of the students study hard. (部分否定) (並非所有的學生都用功。)
  None of the students study hard. (全體否定) (所有學生都不用功。)

- Not both of them are diligent. (部分否定) (並非兩人都勤勞。)
  Neither of them is diligent. (全體否定) (兩個人都不勤勞。)

關鍵試航

1. 有錢人未必快樂。(not always)

_____

2. 好看的食物未必好吃。(not necessarily)

_____

3. 擊敗這名拳擊手相當困難，但並非完全不可能。(not absolutely)

_____

4.她並不是真的那麼笨。(not exactly)

5.不是每個學生都喜歡這個老師。

79 never/not...without + V-ing

You **cannot** take James' book away **without** asking for his permission.

(你不能沒徵求允許就拿走 James 的書。)

用法說明

1 not 和 never 加上 without 形成雙重否定，中文翻譯為「沒有…就不能…」，事實上意味著「要…才…」，因此例句可譯為：你要先徵求 James 的允許才能拿走他的書。

2 若使用的是 never，則可替換為以下句型：

· They never see each other without fighting.

→ Whenever they see each other, they fight.

→ Every time they see each other, they fight. (他們每次一見面就打架。)

學習補給站

★ **never fail to V**　總是能…

fail to V 為表否定之意的片語，在前面加上 never 之後，形成雙重否定，表「一定能…」之意。

· I never fail to see the humor in my father's jokes.

→ I always see the humor in my father's jokes. (我總是能理解我爸爸笑話中的幽默。)

關鍵試航

(每題寫 2 句)

1.那對夫妻一見面就爭吵。

(never...without)

(Whenever)

2. 我看到這張相片就想起我們年輕的日子。

(never...without)

(Every time)

3. 爸爸每次看到我就發脾氣。

(never...without)

(Whenever)

80　not A but B

Mr. Chen is **not** a general **but** a police officer.

(陳先生不是將軍而是警官。)

用法說明

1 本句型中的 but 為對等連接詞，故 A 與 B 應為同詞性的單字、片語或子句。

- Leo is not *fat* but a bit *strong*. (形容詞) (Leo 不胖而是有點壯。)
- The movie does not appeal *to adult females* but *to males and teenagers*.

   (片語) (這部電影吸引的不是成年女性，而是男性及青少年。)
- What matters is not *what you take*, but *what you give*.

   (子句) (重要的不是你得到什麼，而是你付出什麼。)

2 本句型可代換為 B and not A，注意其補語的位置 A 與 B 已互換。

- He is not *a student* but *a teacher*.

   → He is *a teacher*, and not *a student*. (他不是學生而是老師。)

學習補給站

★ **not because A but because B**　　不是因為 A 而是因為 B

- The student was punished not because *he stole the money* but because *he told a lie*.

   (這名學生受懲罰不是因為偷錢而是因為說謊。)

關鍵試航

1. 我叔叔不是商人而是學者。

_____

2. Ken 說：「我不是中國或台灣公民，我是世界公民。」

_____

3. 重要的不是你做什麼，而是你怎麼做。

_____

4. Jenny 受歡迎不是因為她漂亮的外表而是她的好個性。

_____

81   cannot...too...

We **cannot** emphasize the importance of traffic safety **too** much.

(交通安全再強調也不為過。)

用法說明

1 雖然此句型有否定字 (cannot)，但是其含意為「再⋯也不為過」的意思，也就是「愈⋯愈好」，故翻譯為肯定句。

2 可代換為 cannot...enough...。

　　‧ We <u>cannot</u> be <u>too</u> careful in choosing friends.

　　　→ We <u>cannot</u> be careful <u>enough</u> in choosing friends.

　　　　(我們再怎麼謹慎擇友都不為過。)

3 cannot...too many + 複數名詞；cannot...too much + 不可數名詞。

　　‧ It is right that one <u>cannot</u> make <u>too many</u> _friends_. (一個人的朋友愈多愈好是對的。)

4 本句型可和 it is impossible...to...too... 代換。

　　‧ We <u>cannot</u> blame him <u>too</u> much.

　　　→ <u>It is impossible</u> for us <u>to</u> blame him <u>too</u> much. (我們再怎麼怪他也不為過。)

5 本句型亦可用以下的字代換：

　　emphasize...too much → overemphasize　　過度強調

　　estimate...too much → overestimate　　高估

- We cannot *emphasize* its importance <u>too</u> much.
  - → We cannot *overemphasize* its importance.
  - → <u>It is impossible</u> for us <u>to</u> *emphasize* its importance <u>too</u> much.

    (它的重要性再強調也不為過。)

關鍵試航

1. 我們為孩子選擇學校時，再小心也不為過。(cannot...too)

_____

2. 我再怎麼感謝你的善心也不為過。(cannot...too)

_____

3. 我們再怎麼過份重視和平的重要性也不為過。(overvalue)

_____

4. 一個人交愈多朋友愈好。(cannot...too)

_____

5. 我們再強調學英文的重要也不為過。(cannot...too)

_____

82　the last...to V

He is the last person to tell a lie.

(他是最不可能說謊的人。)

用法說明

此句雖然沒有使用否定字詞，但 the last 在字義上有「最後一個」的意思，隱含否定的語意。

- He is <u>the last man</u> to tell the truth.
  - → He is the most *unlikely* man to tell the truth. (他是最不可能說實話的人。)

學習補給站

以下三個句型本身不見否定字，卻都隱含否定之意：

★ **far from...**　一點也不…

- The movie is <u>far from</u> interesting. (這部電影一點都不有趣。)

★ **anything but...**　絕不…

- Taking a plane is <u>anything but</u> dangerous. (搭飛機絕不危險。)

★ **free from...**　沒有…

- I hope my parents can live their lives <u>free from</u> anxieties.

  (我希望我父母可以過沒有憂慮的生活。)

關鍵試航

1. Jessica 是最不可能犯這種錯誤的人。(the last)

_____

2. 我沒有意願幫你的忙。(far from)

_____

3. 陳先生的回答無法令人滿意。(far from)

_____

4. 我覺得他絕非忠誠之人。(anything but)

_____

5. 你不該受責罵。(free from)

_____

Exercises

I. Fill a proper word in each of the following blanks.

    1. 便宜貨不見得省錢。

        Cheap things are _____ _____ economical.

    2. 這個問題絕非簡單。

        This question is _____ _____ easy.

    3. 健康的價值再強調也不為過。

        The value of health _____ _____ overemphasized.

    4. 這些貨物一點都不令人滿意。

        These goods are _____ _____ satisfaction.

    5. Gina 不是為了你而是為了她自己而做。

        Gina did not do so for your sake _____ _____ her own sake.

II. Choose one proper answer.

_____ 1. Not _____ dog can guard the house.

        (A) every   (B) all   (C) many   (D) much

_____ 2. I never visited Tom _____ him at work. He was very diligent.

        (A) without find   (B) without finding (C) but I find   (D) but to find

_____ 3. My sister is _____ one to clean the room.

        (A) the last   (B) a few   (C) last   (D) little

_____ 4. Charlie is not a musician _____ a reporter.

        (A) and   (B) for   (C) but   (D) so

_____ 5. We cannot be _____ careful when crossing the street.

        (A) to   (B) too   (C) so   (D) rather

Note

Unit 12　與讓步有關的句型

83　even if/though

Jack is a very good basketball player **even if** he is not tall.

(即使不高，Jack 是一個很好的籃球球員。)

用法說明

1 even if 和 even though 皆表讓步，但是 even though 的語氣較為強烈。

2 even if 表「讓步」，if 表「條件」，兩者的意思並不相同。

- Even if he shows up in time, I won't speak to him.

  (即使他及時出現，我也不和他說話。)

- If he shows up in time, I will speak to him. (如果他及時出現，我會和他說話。)

3 even if 和 even though 可以搭配與事實相反的假設法：

- Even if I could afford it, I wouldn't buy an expensive diamond ring.

  (即使我負擔得起，我也不買昂貴的鑽戒。)

4 in spite of... = despite... 也有「儘管」之意，是介系詞，之後接名詞。

- Even though she had made constant efforts, she failed the test.

  → In spite of her constant efforts, she failed the test.

  → Despite her constant efforts, she failed the test.

  (儘管不斷地努力，她考試還是不及格。)

5 for/with all 也可表讓步，作「即使」解。

- Even though he was very patient, his students didn't listen to him.

  → In spite of his patience, his students didn't listen to him.

  → For/With all his patience, his students didn't listen to him.

  (即使他很有耐心，學生還是不聽他說話。)

關鍵試航

1. 即使 Bill 這麼說，我們仍然不相信他。(Even if)

2.即使要我花一整天的時間，我也要完成這個報告。(even if)

_____

3.即使我試了，我還是無法改變她的主意。(Even though)

_____

4.儘管她很傷心，她還是假裝開心。(In spite of)

_____

5.儘管她擁有名利，仍舊不開心。(For all)

_____

84　...as/though + S + V

Poor **as he is**, he is happy.　　（他雖然貧窮，但很快樂。）

用法說明

此句型為由 as 或 though 引導，表讓步的倒裝句型。倒裝時，副詞、形容詞、分詞或名詞都可移至句首，但注意名詞移至句首時需將冠詞移除。

- Though/Although he worked *hard*, he didn't pass the exam.
    - → *Hard* as/though he worked, he didn't pass the exam.

        （雖然他很用功，但考試仍不及格。）
- Though/Although Oliver was *a child*, he did a man's job.
    - → *Child* as/though Oliver was, he did a man's job. (移除 child 前面的冠詞 a)

        （雖然 Oliver 是個小孩，卻做男人的工作。）

關鍵試航

1.她雖然年輕，但很有智慧。(as)

_____

2.雖然你讀得很快，你也不可能在一天內讀完這本書。(though)

_____

3.她雖然是個女人，但是在戰場上很勇敢。(as)

_____

4.雖然我的爺爺老了，他仍然活躍。(as)

85　whether...or...

Whether you are happy **or** sad, you should go back to your work.

(無論你是高興或悲傷，都該回去工作。)

用法說明

1 whether...or... 所引導的子句為副詞子句。主要子句的時態若為未來式，副詞子句一般都使用現在式。

- I'll go, <u>whether</u> you *go* with me <u>or</u> *stay* here.

　(不管你要和我一起去或待在此地，我都要走。)

2 若 whether 和 or 欲連接的字詞互為相反之意，則可用 whether...or not。

- <u>Whether</u> you go <u>or not</u>, I'll take the next bus. (不管你是否要去，我都要搭下一班巴士。)

3 若 whether...or... 置於及物動詞之後，則為名詞子句作受詞用。

- I cannot tell <u>whether he is a friend or an enemy</u>. (我無法分辨他是朋友或敵人。)

4 有些常見慣用語省略了 whether 保留 or，形成較簡潔的片語。

- <u>Rain or shine</u>, farmers work hard on the farms. (無論晴雨，農夫都在田裡辛苦工作。)
- <u>Sooner or later</u>, he will find out the fact. (他遲早會發現事實。)
- Everybody has weaknesses, <u>more or less</u>. (每個人或多或少都有弱點。)
- The baby seems happy, <u>asleep or awake</u>. (那個嬰兒無論睡著或醒著，似乎都很開心。)
- <u>Believe it or not</u>, her boyfriend is very old. (信不信由你，她的男友年紀很大。)

關鍵試航

1.無論你是贏或輸，你都會從比賽中學到很多。

2.不管工作是簡單或困難，都要盡力。

3.無論你喜歡與否,你都得學英文。

_____

4.我不知道這個消息是不是真的。

_____

5.信不信由你,Brenda 今天被解雇了。

_____

86 however...may...

However difficult the task **may** be, try to overcome it.

(無論工作可能多困難,設法克服它。)

用法說明

1 however 在此句型裡是複合關係詞,由關係副詞 how 加上 ever 所形成,表示讓步,引導副詞子句。

2 在口語中,可以直接使用一般動詞,不加 may。

  · However delicious the apple seems/may seem, it is poisonous.

   (無論這蘋果看來多可口,它都有毒。)

3 however 之後可以接形容詞或副詞。

  · However *difficult* the task may be, try to overcome it.

   (形容詞) (無論這個工作可能多困難,設法克服它。)

  · However *hard* you may work, you won't pass the difficult test.

   (副詞) (無論你多努力,你都不會通過這個困難的考試。)

學習補給站

複合關係詞表讓步時可以用「no matter + 疑問詞」替換。

however = no matter how   無論如何

whoever = no matter who   無論是誰

whichever = no matter which   無論哪一個

whatever = no matter what   無論什麼

whenever = no matter when　無論何時

wherever = no matter where　無論何地

- Whatever you (may) say, they won't give you any promise.

  → No matter what you (may) say, they won't give you any promise.

  (無論你說什麼，他們都不會給你任何承諾。)

關鍵試航

1. 無論我多累，都得寫功課。

_____

2. 無論誰反對，我都要和 Emily 結婚。

_____

3. 無論她去到哪裡，都受到歡迎。

_____

4. 無論他多努力嘗試，都不會成功。

_____

5. 無論你選哪一個，我都付錢。

_____

87　It is true (that)...but...

It is true that money can buy almost everything, **but** it can't buy true love.

(金錢的確可以買到幾乎一切，但是買不到真愛。)

用法說明

1 It is true that 連接的子句表事實，but 連接的子句則表與該事實相對或不合的情形。

2 下列幾種用法可以互相代換：

- It is true that his story sounds strange, but everyone believes him.

  → Indeed his story sounds strange, but everyone believes him.

  → No doubt his story sounds strange, but everyone believes him.

  → His story may sound strange, but everyone believes him.

  (他的故事的確聽來奇怪，但是每個人都相信他。)

· It is true that she is right, but I just can't accept her opinion.

→ Truly, she is right, but I just can't accept her opinion.

→ No doubt she is right, but I just can't accept her opinion.

→ Indeed she is right, but I just can't accept her opinion.

→ She is right, to be sure, but I just can't accept her opinion.

(她的確是對的，但我就是無法接受她的意見。)

關鍵試航

1.她的確聰明，但沒常識。(true)

_____

2.他的確很富有，但很吝嗇 (stingy)。(true)

_____

3.他的點子的確很棒，但我不認為它行得通 (practicable)。(No doubt)

_____

4.今年的確很熱，但是不如往常潮濕。(Truly)

_____

5.這棟房子真的不貴，但是我不想買。(to be sure)

_____

88 little..., if any

There is **little** money stolen, **if any**.

(如果有錢被偷了，也是很少。)

用法說明

few、little、seldom、rarely 在語意上具有否定意味，經常與 if any 或 if ever 等插入語連用，表示較強烈的讓步。if any 與 if ever 都是省略用法，省略主詞與 be 動詞。

⑴ **little/few..., if any**

· There were <u>few</u> kids infected with the flu last week, <u>if any</u>.

(上星期如果有的話也是極少數的小孩感染流感。)

⑵ **seldom/rarely..., if ever**

・ My mother <u>rarely</u>, <u>if ever</u>, punishes us.

(我媽就算曾經懲罰我們也是很少次。)

學習補給站

以下兩個句型也是表讓步的句型，常放在完整子句之後，表「雖然⋯」之意。

★ **if not...**　　即便不是⋯

・ I've decided to follow my mother's advice, <u>if not</u> the best choice.

(我已經決定要聽從我媽媽的建議，即便不是最佳選擇。)

★ **if anything...**　　即便有⋯

if anything = if there <u>is</u>/<u>are</u> anything 的省略用法。

・ The watch was not expensive——<u>if anything</u>, it only cost me a little money.

(這手錶並不貴——即便有，也只是花了我一點點的錢。)

關鍵試航

1. 如果還有的話，只剩下極少的酒。

_____

2. 即便有，也是極少數人關心空氣污染一事。

_____

3. 他即使曾經有過，也很少約會遲到。

_____

4. 即便不便宜，搭飛機旅行對我們來說比較快。

_____

5. 我買了這個比較便宜的玩偶，即使不是我最喜歡的一個。

_____

Exercises

I. Fill a proper word in each of the following blanks.

1. Young _____ he is, he has much experience and knowledge.

   → He is young, _____ he has much experience and knowledge.

   → _____ he is young, he has much experience and knowledge.

2. In _____ of his parents' sincere advice, he didn't change his mind.

   → With _____ his parents' sincere advice, he didn't change his mind.

   → _____ _____ his parents advised him sincerely, he didn't change his mind.

3. Whatever you _____ say, I won't give it up.

II. Choose one proper answer.

_____ 1. Beautiful as _____, Eva doesn't have any boyfriend.

   (A) she is   (B) is she   (C) her is   (D) is her

_____ 2. There is little food left after the party, _____.

   (A) for all   (B) if not   (C) if any   (D) if possible

_____ 3. Although he is poor, _____.

   (A) but he is diligent   (B) and he never gives up

   (C) he worked day and night   (D) he is happy

_____ 4. _____ the fact that he was ill, he went to school as usual.

   (A) Despite of   (B) Although   (C) In spite of   (D) In case of

_____ 5. _____ you say, I don't believe you anymore.

   (A) How   (B) What

   (C) No matter what   (D) No matter how

Unit 13　　與目的、程度、結果有關的句型

89　so that...__may__/__can__/__will__...

They took preventive measures in advance **so that** they **might** keep the house from severe damage.

(他們事先採取防範的措施，以便防止屋子遭受嚴重損害。)

用法說明

1 本句型表達目的，子句中的 may 可以替換為 can 或 will。若主要子句的時態為過去式，則 that 子句中的 may、can、will 須用 might、could、would 代替。

　　· Practice more <u>so that</u> you <u>can</u> make it perfect. (多練習你就能臻於完美。)

2 本句型中的 so 可以省略，意義不變。

　　· We repaired the computer <u>(so) that</u> we <u>might</u> work with it.

　　　(我們修理電腦，以便能使用它。)

3 本句型可用不定詞片語 so as to... 或 in order to... 加以替換。注意要替換時，主要子句及以 so that 引導的子句之主詞必須相同。

　　· We should walk faster <u>so that</u> we <u>may</u> arrive at school on time.

　　　→ We should walk faster <u>so as to</u> arrive at school on time.

　　　→ We should walk faster <u>in order to</u> arrive at school on time.

　　　(我們應該走快點以便準時到校。)

4 常見片語：for the purpose of + <u>N/V-ing</u> 亦可表目的，作「為了…」解。

　　· He lied <u>for the purpose of concealing</u> his feelings.

　　　→ He lied <u>so that</u> he <u>might</u> conceal his feelings. (他為了掩蓋自己的情感才說謊。)

5 另一常見片語：with <u>a view</u>/<u>an eye</u> to... 也是表達目的，注意此時的 to 是介系詞，故其後接名詞或動名詞。

　　· She worked day and night <u>with a view to supporting</u> her family.

　　　→ She worked day and night <u>so that</u> she <u>could</u> support her family.

　　　(她日夜工作以便養家活口。)

關鍵試航

1. 我們必須盡全力，這樣我們才會贏。(so that...may)

2. 你應該每天讀英文報紙，以便使你的英文進步。(so that...may)

3. 那些露營者 (campers) 生火以便煮晚餐。(so that...may)

4. 為了防止作弊，我們老師上週訂定了一條新規定。(so as to)

5. 為了學畫，他到巴黎去。(for the purpose of)

90　lest...(should) + 原形 V

Take an umbrella with you **lest** it **should rain**.

(隨身帶把傘以免下雨。)

用法說明

1 本句型所表達的是否定的目的，句型中的助動詞一定是 should，且可省略，故 lest 引導的子句中不論主詞為何，皆使用原形動詞。

- Hand in your assignment on time <u>lest</u> you <u>(should)</u> *be* punished.

  (準時交作業以免受罰。)

2 類似句型：for fear (that)...<u>should</u>/<u>might</u>/<u>would</u>... 可以互為替換。注意：此句型中的助動詞不可省略。

- She went to bed early <u>lest</u> she get up late the next morning.

  → She went to bed early <u>for fear (that)</u> she <u>would</u> get up late the next morning.

  (她早點就寢以免隔天睡太晚。)

3 若 for fear (that)... 的主要子句與從屬子句的主詞一致時，可替換為 for fear of + V-ing。

- Mrs. Tinker refused to attend the party <u>for fear that</u> she might run into her ex-husband.

→ Mrs. Tinker refused to attend the party <u>for fear of running</u> into her ex-husband.

(Tinker 夫人拒絕參加舞會，免得碰到前夫。)

4 以上句型可與 in case... 替換，而此用法中的從屬子句不須特定用 should 等助動詞。

- Don't help him so often <u>lest</u> he <u>(should)</u> have excuses again.

→ Don't help him so often <u>in case</u> he <u>has/should have</u> excuses again.

(別經常幫他，免得他再有藉口。)

關鍵試航

1. 我靠邊站以免擋到那位老太太的路。(lest...should)

_____

2. 請不要打開電視以免吵醒嬰兒。(lest...should)

_____

3. 記得帶地圖以免迷路。(in case)

_____

4. 別靠近籠子以免老虎咬你。(for fear that)

_____

5. 我每天早起，惟恐錯過火車。(for fear of)

_____

91　so...that...

The girl is **so** attractive **that** she is welcomed everywhere.

(那個女孩如此迷人以致於到處受歡迎。)

用法說明

1 so...that... 與 such...that... 和 so...as to... 的用法比較：

⑴ **so...that...**　　so 之後可接形容詞或副詞

- The novel is <u>so</u> *interesting* <u>that</u> many teenage readers love it.

(這本小說是如此地有趣，以致於許多青少年讀者喜愛它。)

⑵ **such...that...**　　such 之後接形容詞＋名詞

- It is such *an interesting novel* that many teenage readers love it.

  (這是一本如此有趣的小說，以致於很多青少年讀者喜愛它。)

(3) **so...as to...**　to 之後接原形動詞

- The novel is so interesting as to *attract* many teenage readers.

  (這本小說是如此地有趣，以致於吸引了許多青少年讀者。)

2 so...that... 的主要子句與 that 引導的從屬子句主詞一致時，可與 so...as to... 互換：

- She is so rich that she bought an island in the Pacific Ocean.

  → She is so rich as to buy an island in the Pacific Ocean.

  (她很有錢，所以在太平洋買了一座島。)

關鍵試航

1. Sandra 說話速度很快，我們都跟不上她。(so...that)

   _____

2. 昨天天氣很好，所以我們去野餐。(such...that)

   _____

3. 他太笨了，所以對她說實話。(so...as to)

   _____

4. 她病得如此嚴重，以致於無法工作。(so...that)

   _____

5. 這部車太貴了，以致於 Larry 沒辦法買它。(such...that)

   _____

92　too...to...

The manager is **too** busy **to** take a break.

(這位經理太忙而無法休息。)

用法說明

1 本句型其實是上一個句型的延伸，too...to... = so...that...not...。

- I was too busy to talk to you.

→ I was <u>so</u> busy <u>that</u> I could<u>n't</u> talk to you. (我太忙以致於無法和你說話。)

· She was <u>too</u> conceited <u>to</u> win the game.

→ She was <u>so</u> conceited <u>that</u> she could<u>n't</u> win the game. (她太自負而無法贏得比賽。)

2 可以在不定詞之前加上 for + 人，此時的人為不定詞的意義主詞，也就是動作的產生者。

· The task is <u>too</u> difficult <u>for him</u> <u>to</u> complete.

(這任務對他來說太難了，以致於無法完成。)

關鍵試航

1. 這杯水太燙了，我無法喝下去。(too...to)

_____

2. 那輛車距離太遠，我看不到。(too...to)

_____

3. 這個箱子太重，他獨自一人扛不動。(too...to)

_____

4. 她太震驚而說不出話。(too...to)

_____

5. 我昨天太晚回家而沒有看到最喜歡的電視節目。(too...to)

_____

93　..., so that...

He put on the raincoat, **so that** he wouldn't get wet.

(他穿上雨衣，所以不會淋濕。)

用法說明

1 so that 之前有逗點時，意思等於 so，表「所以」之意，用以表示「結果」；而句型 **89 so that...may...** 則表示「目的」。

· He walked faster, <u>so (that)</u> he would catch the bus. (他走得較快些，所以趕上了公車。)

· He walked faster <u>so that</u> he <u>might</u> catch the bus. (為了要趕上公車，他走得較快些。)

2 ..., (and) so... 以及 ..., and therefore... 皆可表相同的意思。

- Claire worked hard, <u>so that</u> she passed the exam smoothly.

  → Claire worked hard, <u>(and) so</u> she passed the exam smoothly.

  → Claire worked hard, <u>and therefore</u> she passed the exam smoothly.

  (Claire 很努力，因此順利通過考試。)

3 so that...<u>may/can/will</u> 與 ..., so that... 和 so...that... 的分別。

- He spoke loudly <u>so that</u> we could hear him clearly.

  (目的) (為了讓我們聽清楚，他說得很大聲。)

  He spoke loudly, <u>so that</u> we could hear him clearly.

  (結果) (他說得很大聲，因此我們聽得很清楚。)

  He spoke <u>so</u> loudly <u>that</u> we could hear him clearly.

  (程度) (他說得如此大聲，以致於我們可以聽得清楚。)

關鍵試航

1. 我的車子拋錨了，因此今天早上我走路上班。(..., so that)

   _____

2. Becky 打電話給她的父母，因此他們知道她已經到達宿舍了。(..., so that)

   _____

3. 我的父親年輕時很努力工作，因此賺了一筆財富。(..., and so)

   _____

4. 為了能準時上課，我搭了計程車。(so that...may)

   _____

5. 他太累了，所以無法專心於他的作業。(so...that)

   _____

94 ...only to...

Our team practiced day and night **only to** lose the game again.

(我們這一隊日夜練習結果又再度輸了。)

用法說明

1 only to 所引導的不定詞片語視同副詞片語，表示「令人不悅，失望的結果」。須注意的是，主要子句與此不定詞片語的主詞是相同的。

- He went to the zoo with excitement, <u>only to</u> *see* nothing special.

  （他很興奮地去動物園，結果沒看到什麼特別的。）

2 不定詞表示結果，常見於一些慣用語，舉例如下：

★ **grow up to be...**　長大之後成為⋯

- Daniel <u>grew up to be</u> a physicist and won the Nobel Prize.

  （Daniel 長大成為物理學家並獲得了諾貝爾獎。）

★ **awake to find...**　醒來發現⋯

- The old woman <u>awoke to find</u> her purse stolen.

  （老婦人醒過來時發現她的錢包被偷了。）

★ **never to...**　從此不⋯

- The man made up his mind <u>never to</u> cheat on his wife.

  （那個人下定決心絕不對妻子不忠。）

關鍵試航

1. 我很努力結果又再度失敗。

_____

2. 我們去年去了北極 (the North Pole)，結果沒發現任何令人興奮的事。

_____

3. 小男孩已經花了兩小時在功課上，結果只完成其中的一半。

_____

4. 我醒來時發現自己躺在醫院。

_____

5. 她二十歲時決定在賺到一百萬之前絕不回家。

_____

95 to one's surprise

To my surprise, he became a martial artist.

(令我驚訝的是,他成為一個武術家。)

用法說明

1「to + 所有格 + 表感情的抽象名詞」形成副詞片語,表示「某事造成某人的情緒反應」。類似的常見片語有:

★ **to one's regret** 令…遺憾的是

- To Dick's regret, his parents could not attend his college graduation ceremony.

(令 Dick 感到遺憾的是,他的父母無法參加他的大學畢業典禮。)

★ **to one's shock** 令…震驚的是

- To our shock, the cop turned out to be a drug dealer.

(令我們震驚的是,那個警察原來是毒販。)

★ **to one's joy** 令…喜悅的是

- To his parents' joy, Jack won the championship. (令 Jack 父母喜悅的是,他得了冠軍。)

2 強調此片語時,可以在名詞之前加上 great,即 to one's great...,或在不定詞 to 之前加上 much,即 much to one's...。

- To my great disappointment, you lost the race. (令我大失所望的是,你賽跑輸了。)
- Much to Felicia's excitement, her boyfriend held a birthday party for her.

(令 Felicia 興奮的是,她男友為她辦了場生日派對。)

關鍵試航

1. 令 Henry 驚訝的是,她女兒決定要跟一個大她二十歲的男人結婚。

_____

2. 令我訝異的是,她突然在眾人面前放聲大笑。(astonishment)

_____

3. 令我們喜悅的是,地主隊 (host team) 昨天贏得了比賽。

_____

4.令我大大地鬆了一口氣的是，所有問題都已經解決了。(relief)

_____

5.令她非常憂傷的是，她的祖父上週去世了。(sorrow)

_____

Exercises

I. Choose one proper answer.

_____ 1. Martha is _____ clever _____ she learns everything quickly.

(A) so; that   (B) such a; that   (C) so; as   (D) such an; that

_____ 2. She is _____ a charming girl that she is popular at school.

(A) so   (B) such   (C) as   (D) how

_____ 3. It was _____ day that we all went out for a picnic.

(A) so fine   (B) so a fine   (C) such fine   (D) such a fine

_____ 4. Come closer _____ you can see the details of the painting.

(A) in order to   (B) so that   (C) so as to   (D) and this

_____ 5. You should keep milk in a refrigerator _____ it should spoil soon.

(A) in order   (B) so that   (C) lest   (D) too

_____ 6. David studies English every day _____ passing the test.

(A) in order that   (B) with a view to   (C) lest he should   (D) so that

_____ 7. _____ my relief, my dog finally recovered from the illness.

(A) In   (B) For   (C) To   (D) By

_____ 8. I'm sorry I was _____ tired to attend the party.

(A) so   (B) very   (C) such   (D) too

Unit 14　特殊句型

96　So + 助動詞/be 動詞 + S

They will go to the World Cup by air. **So will I.**

(他們會搭飛機去參加世界盃足球賽。我也會。)

1 本句型用於表達相同或類似的情況，so 之後形成倒裝句型。如果前句使用 be 動詞，倒裝句中應將主詞置於 be 動詞之後。若前句使用一般動詞，so 之後先放助動詞 do/does/did，再放主詞。若前句有 can、will、could、would 等助動詞，則在 so 之後重複助動詞再加主詞。

- He is an engineer. So is my brother. (他是工程師。我哥哥也是。)
- He goes to work by car. So do I. (他開車上班。我也是。)
- He can swim. So can Mary. (他會游泳。Mary 也會。)

2 若前句為否定句時則 so 改為 neither/nor。

- He can't swim. Neither can I.

  → He can't swim. I can't, either. (他不會游泳。我也不會。)

- She isn't a reporter. Nor am I.

  → She isn't a reporter. I'm not, either. (她不是記者，我也不是。)

當 so 之後未形成倒裝時，So + S + V 的句型表示贊同對方的意見，此時的 so 有 yes 的意思。

- He takes everything seriously. So do I.

  (他認真看待每一件事。我也是。)

- "He takes everything seriously." "So he does."

  (「他認真看待每一件事。」「是的，他是如此。」)

關鍵試航

1. 我喜歡茶勝過咖啡。Tom 也是。

_____

2. Lucy 是大學生。我也是。

_____

3. 我不會說日文。他也不會。

_____

4. A:「你似乎是個音樂家。」B:「是的,我是。」

_____

97 suggest that + S + (should) + 原形 V

The doctor **suggested that** my father **(should) give up** smoking.
(醫生建議我爸爸應該戒菸。)

用法說明

1 that 子句中的助動詞 should 可以省略,主詞之後直接接原形動詞。

- I suggested that he <u>leave</u> as soon as possible. (我建議他儘早離開。)
- My net pal suggested that we <u>meet</u> in front of the train station.

  (我網友建議我們在車站前會面。)

2 除了 suggest,還有許多用法相同的動詞。此類動詞多半與意志有關,後接 that 引導的名詞子句。此類動詞可略分為五種:

⑴提議:suggest、propose 等

- He <u>proposed that</u> the meeting <u>(should) be</u> postponed until next Friday.

  (他提議將會議延期至下星期五。)

⑵命令:order、command 等

- The judge <u>ordered that</u> the prisoner <u>(should) be</u> set free. (法官命令釋放犯人。)

⑶要求:ask、request、require、demand 等

- We <u>request that</u> all members <u>(should) attend</u> the rehearsal.

  (我們要求所有的成員參加這次的預演。)

(4)建議：recommend、advise 等

• Do you <u>recommend that</u> every high school graduate <u>(should) attend</u> college?

(你會建議每個高中畢業生都去唸大學嗎？)

(5)主張：urge、insist 等

• John's father <u>insisted that</u> he <u>(should) go</u> to college.

(John 的父親堅持要他上大學。)

關鍵試航

1. 她要求那家報社公開道歉。(demand)

_____

2. 國王下令處死那名士兵。(order)

_____

3. 在上次的討論中，我堅持他辭去主席一職。(insist)

_____

98 Why not...?

Why not attend the graduation ceremony in person?

(你為什麼不親自參加畢業典禮？)

用法說明

1 本句型為 Why don't you...? 的省略句，所以 why not 之後必接原形動詞。

• <u>Why don't you</u> go with us?

→ <u>Why not</u> go with us? (你為什麼不跟我們一塊兒去？)

2 作為答覆時的意義：

(1)表質疑對方否定的提議

• "You shouldn't stand here." "<u>Why not?</u>"

(「你不應該站在這裡。」「為什麼不可以？」)

(2)表贊同他人肯定的提議

• "Let's go get something to eat." "<u>Why not?</u>"

(「我們去找點東西吃吧！」「有何不可？」)

學習補給站

★ **How come...?** 為什麼… (其後接直述句而非疑問句)

· **How come** you were late again?

→ Why were you late again? (你為什麼又遲到了？)

★ **Why is/was it (that)...?** 為什麼…

· **Why is it (that)** she doesn't show up?

→ Why doesn't she show up? (她為什麼沒出現？)

關鍵試航

1. 為什麼不問她要不要外出用餐？(Why not)

2. 為何你不請他幫忙？(How come)

3. 「不要把你的車停在這裡！」「為何不可？」

4. 「我們接受她的提議吧！」「有何不可？」

5. 他為什麼拋棄妻兒子女？(Why was it)

99 as it is

I'm in enough trouble **as it is**.

(我的麻煩已經夠多了。)

用法說明

as it is 在句中的位置不同其意義亦隨之改變，說明如下：

1 出現在句尾，表示依照目前的狀態，意為「已經、早就是」(= already)；若 be 動詞改為 was，則表示當時的狀態。

· The situation is in a mess **as it is**. (現在的局勢已經夠亂了。)

・ You didn't seem to have to apologize <u>as it was</u>. (照當時的狀況你似乎不必道歉。)

2 出現在句首，表示實際的狀態，意為「實際上、事實上」(= in reality; in fact)。

・ If I had enough money, I would buy the car. <u>As it is</u>, I can't afford it.

　　→ If I had enough money, I would buy the car. In reality, I can't afford it.

　　　(如果我有錢就會買車，但實際上我無法負擔。)

3 作插入語，強調一如現狀。

・ The name of our country, <u>as it is</u>, is Republic of China.

　(我們國家目前的名稱是中華民國。)

學習補給站

★ **as it were**　　好比是；可以說是 (通常作為插入語)

・ My grandma, <u>as it were</u>, is an eternal beauty. (我祖母可以說是永遠的美人。)

關鍵試航

1. 就讓這件事保持現狀吧！

_____

2. 別再爭吵了。目前的狀況已經夠糟糕了。

_____

3. 如果我是警察，我現在就會逮捕他。但實際上，我不能這麼做。

_____

4. 目前的法律是不夠嚴厲的。

_____

5. Alice 專注於科學研究，可以說是現代的居禮夫人 (Madame Curie)。

_____

100 疑問詞 + **on earth...?**

What on earth are you doing?

(你到底在做什麼？)

用法說明

1 疑問詞之後加上 on earth，用來加強語氣，譯為「到底、究竟」。

- Where on earth did you go last night? (你昨晚到底去哪裡了？)
- How on earth did you get into the trouble? (你究竟是如何捲入這個麻煩？)

2 on earth 亦可以 in the world 取代。

- Who in the world are you looking for? (你到底在找誰？)
- When in the world will you come back? (你究竟何時才會回來？)

學習補給站

以下兩種句型也是常見的加強語氣用法：

★ **the very + N** 正是，就是

- Harry is the very man that I want to marry. (Harry 就是我想要嫁的人。)

★ **do/does/did + 原形 V** 的確

- We did invite the Wang family to dinner.

  → We really invited the Wang family to dinner. (我們真的有邀請王家一家人吃晚餐。)

關鍵試航

1. 你到底需要多少錢？

   _____

2. 他們昨天究竟為什麼對你大吼大叫？

   _____

3. Martin 博士究竟現在要去哪裡？

   _____

4. 這就是我昨天帶回家的小狗。

   _____

5. 我的確忘了有關你的邀約。

   _____

101 省略句

You can leave early if you want **to**.

(如果你想早點離開，你可以先離開。)

用法說明

1 含有不定詞的句構中，若不定詞之後的動詞與前面的動詞相同時，只保留不定詞中的 to，而重複的字可省略。

- You may call me Mike if you want to call me Mike.
    - → You may call me Mike if you want to. (如果你想叫我 Mike 就這麼叫吧。)

2 對等連接詞 and 連接兩個對等子句，若動詞相同時，第二個動詞可省略。

- Jane's father is a doctor, and her mother is a nurse.
    - → Jane's father is a doctor, and her mother a nurse.

      (Jane 的父親是醫生，母親是護士。)

3 when、while、if、once、unless、though 等連接詞所引導的副詞子句中，若主詞與主要子句相同時，可以省略，其後動詞改為現在分詞，若為 be 動詞，則可省略。

- Joe always calls me when he needs help.
    - → Joe always calls me when needing help. (Joe 需要幫忙的時候總是打電話給我。)
- You can call the police for help if you are in trouble.
    - → You can call the police for help if in trouble.

      (如果遇到麻煩，你可以報警尋求協助。)

4 同位語多由 who is 或 which is 引導的形容詞子句簡化而來，who 和 which 省略之後，is 可改為 being 或省略。

- Eddie's girlfriend, who is my coworker, is capable and amiable.
    - → Eddie's girlfriend, (being) my coworker, is capable and amiable.

      (Eddie 的女友是我的工作夥伴，能幹且藹可親。)

關鍵試航

1. 如果你想哭就哭吧！

2. 有各種大小的船。有些大,有些小。

3. 漫畫書不僅吸引小孩也吸引大人。(appeal to)

4. 雖然他們很貧窮,但過著幸福的日子。

5. White 先生的女兒 Sonia 昨天結婚了。

I. Fill a proper word in each of the following blanks.

1. 他現在不富裕，我也不是。

   He is not rich, _____ _____ I.

2. 我必須看到事物的原貌。

   I must see things _____ _____ _____ .

3. 為何不過來我這兒喝杯咖啡？

   _____ _____ come over to my place to have a cup of coffee?

II. Choose one proper answer.

_____ 1. I have _____ the money nor the ability to set up a new business.

    (A) none   (B) or   (C) either   (D) neither

_____ 2. The emperor ordered that the killer _____ put to death.

    (A) were   (B) be   (C) was   (D) is

_____ 3. _____ in prison, Valentine fell in love with a young girl who visited him.

    (A) Where   (B) What   (C) While   (D) Why

Note

解答

1
1. It is possible for us to be late.
2. It is easy for Tony's team to win the game.
3. It is foolish of the police to do so.
4. It is no use arguing with our parents.

2
1. I found it impossible to complete the work in time.
2. We all feel it a pity that you leave the company.
3. Bad weather made it hard for the climbers to reach the top of the mountain.
4. My father makes it a rule to keep early hours.
5. I take it for granted that Dr. Jones will attend the meeting on time.

3
1. It seems/appears that you are not happy at all to be with me.
2. It seems/appears that you are all wrong.
3. It seems/appears that our manager is satisfied with the dress.
4. It is said that the old man was a millionaire.

4
1. It took three years to build the bridge.
2. It took him a whole life to carry out his dream.
3. It cost me five hundred dollars to have the computer fixed.
4. It takes great patience to train these animals.
5. It takes some courage to make a speech in public.

5
1. It never occurred to us that he would tell a lie.
2. It occurred to me that I should call my parents right away.
3. It struck Fred that he should keep the secret.

6
1. It doesn't matter to the competitors whether their coaches will show up or not.
2. It matters little whether you agree to my proposal or not.
3. It hardly matters to me whether she is the president's daughter or not.
4. It doesn't matter whether the result is good or bad.
5. It makes no difference to me whether you go to school or go to work.

7
1. It is Mary that/who is wrong.
2. It was last weekend that he left for the U.S.
3. It was because the female dancer came down with the flu that she lost the opportunity to win first prize.

4. It was the price your boss offered which surprised me.

5. What is it that Dr. Wang is working on?

Exercises

I. 1. is, said, to, have, been

2. without, saying, that 3. it

II. 1.D 2.B 3.D 4.C 5.C

6.D 7.D 8.A 9.A 10.D

Unit 2

8 1. I have two sisters. One studies in college, and the other (studies) in senior high school.

2. Only one student passed the exam, and the others failed.

---

9 1. Work and play are both necessary; the one gives us achievement, and the other rest.

2. Scene and scenery both mean beautiful sights; the former is a countable noun, and the latter is an uncountable noun.

3. You can get to Kaohsiung by plane or by train, but that is much faster than this.

---

10 1. There are many children in the park. Some are flying kites, and the others are riding bikes.

2. Some metals are magnetic, and others are not.

3. There are many students in the gym.

Some are playing basketball, and all the others are playing table tennis.

4. He has three cellphones. One is red, another is black, and the other is silver.

5. Some food tastes good, and some bad.

---

11 1. To know is one thing, and to practice is another.

2. Knowing and practicing are two different things.

3. Understanding is different from realization.

4. The girls sat on the chairs, facing one another.

---

12 1. He has lived in the mansion by himself since his wife passed away.

2. Can you afford the tuition by yourself?

3. He bought a car for himself.

4. The dog opened the door by itself.

5. Ambition is not bad in itself.

---

13 1. The population of northern Taiwan is larger than that of southern Taiwan.

2. Cars in the 20th century were quite different from those in modern times.

3. You must hand in your answer sheet, and that immediately.

4. The Dragon Boat Festival is on the fifth of May on the lunar calendar; that is, this Wednesday.

Exercises

I. 1. by 2. by 3. in 4. for 5. that 6. those

II. 1.B 2.C 3.C 4.C 5.D
6.C 7.B 8.A 9.D

Unit 3

14 1. They used to go to church on Sundays.

2. I used to stay up studying when I was in college.

3. I remember there used to be an Italian restaurant on the corner.

4. My father used to swim in the morning.

5. My father is used to swimming in the morning.

---

15 1. You'd better be quiet now.

2. We'd better not cancel the meeting.

3. For the sake of health, you may as well quit smoking and drinking.

4. I might as well take a nap at home as see a dull movie.

5. She may well be proud of her only son.

---

16 1. My classmate may have taken my umbrella by mistake.

2. He should have arrived at the station by now, but he has not turned up yet.

3. You need not have come to the office so early.

4. I could have picked you up, but I didn't feel well suddenly.

---

17 1. I would like to send this package by airmail.

2. I would like a sandwich and a cup of coffee.

3. Would you like another piece of cake?

4. I would like you to call her in person.

5. I guess she'd like to be alone for a while.

Exercises

I. 1. need, not, have, lent 2. better, have
3. may, as, well 4. used, to, making

II. 1.D 2.A 3.C 4.D 5.B
6.A 7.B 8.B 9.D 10.D

Unit 4

18 1. Hearing the bad news, he was quite at a loss for what to do.

2. The problem is how to explain to the boss that the conference was not successful.

3. My mother doesn't know how to use a computer.

4. Louis doesn't know what to say in the meeting.

5. Amy has no idea whether to trust a person with bad records or not.

---

19 1. The swimming contest is to be held on the weekend.

2. You are to pay off your debt by the end of the year.

3. Not a single clue was to be found in his office, I suppose.

4. Due to the carelessness in the process, the experiment was to fail.

5. If you are to succeed, you should do your best.

20
1. From John's complexion, he seems to have caught a cold.
2. Based on this picture, Joy seemed to have been a singer while young.
3. My mother told me that Grandma seemed to have been a beauty while young.
4. It seems that they had fun at the dinner party.
5. Tina wished to have met Daniel when she was studying in the U.S.

21
1. The police saw the thief run away.
2. Tom heard someone cry last night.
3. The student's performance made the teacher feel disappointed.
4. Kelly's mother let her travel in Europe alone.
5. All the students at this school are made to memorize new words every day.

22
1. Most tourists cannot but admire the beautiful sight.
2. After hearing Tim's joke, I cannot help bursting out laughing.
3. When the host announced Stacy was the winner, she couldn't help but cry.
4. The criminal could not choose but tell the truth.
5. The old man did nothing but complain

about the bad service in the restaurant.

23
1. How did you come to be acquainted with your girlfriend?
2. How did you get to play the flute at last?
3. Believe it or not, the rumor will prove to be false.
4. The basketball team of our school turned out to lose the game.
5. The prisoner managed to escape from the jail.

24
1. The car accident has something to do with drunk driving.
2. Wealth and fame have little to do with happiness.
3. The disaster had nothing to do with the weather.
4. Nature has much to do with animals and plants.
5. You have to do with the problem, because it's your responsibility.

25
1. Anyone who works hard is likely to succeed.
2. We are anxious to hear good news about you.
3. Whenever he gets angry, he is liable to shout at others.
4. I am ready to move to my new house.
5. As long as you stick to your research, you are sure to succeed.

26
1. Adam has the kindness to lend me his motorcycle.
2. She had the fortune to win first prize.
3. The man had the boldness to jump into the river to save the drowning boy.
4. Iris is so silly as to believe Jack would marry her.

27
1. To tell the truth, I was against the plan in the beginning.
2. Strange to say, the door opened by itself.
3. To do Jack justice, he is the most honest man I've ever known.
4. The old woman sitting at the information desk is, so to speak, a walking dictionary.
5. To make matters worse, it began to rain as soon as we arrived at the destination.

Exercises

I. 1.C 2.B 3.C 4.D 5.A
   6.A 7.D 8.A 9.B

II. 1. Not a thing was to be seen
   2. had me translate the book
   3. couldn't but sigh when hearing
   4. be sure to warm
   5. come to realize the importance of being honest

Unit 5

28
1. Arriving at the airport, Karen called her parents.
2. Having nothing to do, she went to bed earlier.
3. Turning left, you will see the MRT station.
4. Understanding what you say, I do not agree with you.
5. Waving her hand, Joy said goodbye to her parents.

29
1. Seen from a distance, the mountain looks like a dog.
2. Having finished his homework, Gary went swimming.
3. Compared with her colleagues, Sherry is an earnest worker.
4. Not knowing what to say, I kept silent in the meeting.
5. Not having caught the flag, the catcher fell into the water.

30
1. Judging from grammar rules, this sentence is not correct.
2. The vacation being over, the laborers came back to their positions of work right away.
3. Considering the budget, the project is not likely to be carried out.
4. Speaking of playing tennis, Arthur is said to be second to none.
5. Generally speaking, boys are naughtier than girls.

31 1. There were many people waiting for the bus at seven o'clock in the morning.

2. There was a cold wind blowing from the sea.

3. There is only a one-week vacation left before his departure.

---

32 1. Vicky read the story to the children with her eyes shining.

2. Don't talk with your mouth full of food.

3. He read the letter from his son with his glasses on.

4. She told me a sad story with tears in her eyes.

5. Leo rushed into the classroom with breakfast in his hand.

---

33 1. I had my purse stolen on a crowded bus.

2. I want to have the washing machine repaired.

3. The old man had his only house burnt in the fire.

4. I want to have someone wash my car.

5. The bookstore will get your book sent off by tomorrow.

---

34 1. Can you make yourself understood in English?

2. My father left the engine running when he was taking a nap in the car yesterday.

3. Now we have a visitor staying here with us to discuss the issue.

4. I could not make myself heard because of the noise.

5. You had better have your telephone fixed.

Exercises

I. 1. is someone waiting for you

2. with his heart beating fast

3. my father had me taking

4. there was a purse left

II. 1.C 2.B 3.C 4.B 5.D

6.C 7.D 8.A 9.D 10.A

Unit 6

35 1. On discovering the truth, the secretary reported it to the employer.

2. On seeing the beehive, he ran away.

3. On graduating from college, she got married.

4. On my return home, I threw myself onto the bed.

5. You must be careful in crossing a busy street.

---

36 1. There is no escaping from the trap.

2. There is no knowing what will/is going to happen tomorrow.

3. There is nothing like my mother's beef noodles.

4. There is no use regretting what has been done.

5. There is no use arguing with the stubborn man.

37

1. Would you mind <u>doing me a favor/giving me a hand</u>?

2. It is too crowded here. Would you mind moving over a bit?

3. Would you mind <u>my/me</u> smoking here?

4. "Would you mind calling back later?" "Not at all."

5. Do you mind <u>my/me</u> coming to your birthday party?

38

1. I feel like dancing with him to the music.

2. I don't feel like <u>taking a walk/a walk</u> tonight.

39

1. The retired general is in the habit of jogging in the morning.

2. I make it a rule to take a bath before <u>sleeping/going to bed</u>.

3. We used to talk about the future.

4. My uncle used to drink a cup of coffee in the morning.

40

1. Most people are not <u>used/accustomed</u> to sleeping during the day.

2. You will soon be <u>used/accustomed</u> to such a political atmosphere.

3. I got <u>used/accustomed</u> to studying in the library alone.

4. She used to complain about everything.

5. All of us are looking forward to seeing you again.

41

1. Nobody can prevent me from marrying her.

2. My bad cold prevented me from attending the meeting.

3. Laura's self-esteem kept her from bursting into tears.

4. Don't hinder your daughter from carrying out her dream.

5. Why didn't you stop her (from) getting into trouble?

42

1. When it comes to playing the piano, Monica is second to none in her class.

2. The boy came near being hit by the bus.

3. He has difficulty (in) solving the problem.

4. The students are busy (in) preparing for the final exams.

5. What do you say to having dinner together?

Exercises

I. 1. from, going 2. <u>Upon/On</u>, seeing
   3. no, denying 4. How, about, seeing

II. 1.C 2.D 3.D 4.D 5.D
   6.B 7.A 8.D 9.C 10.B

III. 1. <u>Upon/On</u>, seeing 2. nothing, like
   3. When, it, comes, to

Unit 7

43
1. I owe what I am to my parents.

2. After studying abroad for ten years, Tony is not what he used to be.

3. A man's happiness depends on what he is rather than what he has.

4. He spent what he had in one night.

44
1. Our manager lacks what we call a sense of humor.

2. Her husband is what one calls a typical English gentleman.

3. My landlord is what you call a selfish man.

4. His elder brother graduated from what is called the best college.

5. I think the so-called educational reform is to raise the standard of education.

45
1. This book is such an easy one as I thought.

2. This piece of news is such a fact as the media has predicted before.

3. Jack likes to take exercise, such as playing basketball and swimming.

46
1. There is scarcely a man but loves his own family.

2. There is no one but knows how to use a cellphone.

3. There is hardly a Chinese but knows the Great Wall.

4. It never rains but pours in my hometown.

5. There is no student but knows the principal.

47
1. All Alisa has to do now is (to) study hard.

2. All we can do now is (to) wait for Mr. Thomas' arrival.

3. All you should do now is (to) wish me luck.

4. In that game, the best thing I could do was (to) cheer you on.

5. All I know is that Abel has nothing to do with the theft.

48
1. This is why Joe is still angry with me.

2. He didn't know your address. That's why he didn't pay you a visit.

3. This is the reason (that) we cannot attend the meeting.

4. Is that how you solve a problem?

5. That is the way (that) Jessie communicates with others.

49
1. He gave his wife what money he had.

2. I spent what time I could spare on the study of social phenomena.

3. Buck told his boss what ideas he had in his mind.

4. I would like to do what little service I can do for you.

50
1. Alina has two daughters, who major in

law.

2. This is Taipei 101, which is designed by a world-famous architect.

3. Some people don't eat breakfast, which does harm to health.

4. The king was betrayed by his men who he thought were loyal to him.

5. She is the best person that I know is suitable for the mission.

Exercises

I. 1. the, way 2. no, but, moved

3. such, as 4. be, what

II. 1.A 2.A 3.B 4.B 5.D 6.A 7.A 8.C

Unit 8

51 1. Mother had no sooner heard the bad news than she turned pale.

2. As soon as I left home, it began to rain.

3. No sooner had my brother come home than he went to sleep without taking a bath.

4. Hardly had the little girl seen the barking dog when she burst into tears.

5. Scarcely had the teacher dismissed the class before the students rushed out of the classroom.

---

52 1. Joannie had not graduated from college long before she found a job.

2. We had not waited long before the train came.

3. They had not been married a month

before they began to quarrel.

4. It was not long before the rumor proved to be false.

5. It will not be long before the company starts to promote its new computer.

---

53 1. We don't know the value of health until we lose it.

2. Not until I got home did I find that I lost my umbrella.

3. It was not until Tom told her that she knew her boyfriend's situation in America.

4. Judy didn't leave the platform until the train was out of her sight.

---

54 1. It has been more than six years since the supermarket was established.

2. Two years have passed since my grandfather fell ill.

---

55 1. Every time my grandmother comes, she brings me presents.

2. Each time we play chess, my father wins.

3. The next time we meet, Tom will bring me the documents I need.

4. Pablo was just five years old the last time I saw him.

5. I hope it will stop raining by the time we arrive at the destination.

Exercises

I. 1. not, until, that 2. has, been

II. 1.D 2.C 3.A 4.D 5.B 6.C

Unit 9

56
1. If a big earthquake should occur, what shall we do?
2. If anyone should call Peter up, say that he will be back tomorrow.
3. If I should be late for school again, I would be willing to receive the teacher's punishment.
4. If you were to join our team, we would be the champion.
5. If the sun were to rise in the west, Maggie would change her mind to marry you.

57
1. If it were not for the air, we could not live.
2. If it were not for the boss' advice, my project would not succeed.
3. If it had not been for the professor's support two years ago, we might have given up the plan.
4. Were it not for music, the world would be dull.
5. Had it not been for your parents' presence yesterday, I would have punished you.

58
1. Without the wind, today would be a pleasant day.

2. But for the rain, we could go on a picnic.
3. But for the storm, we would have arrived at the destination.
4. With your support, I could succeed.
5. With the telephone, you could contact your friends worldwide easily.

59
1. If only I could play the piano as well as Beethoven.
2. If only the plane had landed on time.
3. Would to God that I were young again.
4. How I wish I had a car of my own.
5. Oh, that I could travel around the world.

60
1. It is time we were leaving.
2. It is time you finished your homework for the winter vacation.
3. It is high time you went to work.
4. It is about time we prepared for the exam.
5. It is time for you to hand in the answer sheets.

61
1. Suppose that you were the boss, how would you deal with the event?
2. Supposing (that) you are late, what excuse will you have?
3. Suppose that you fail the exams, how will you explain to your parents?
4. You may go anywhere on condition that you'll come back home by ten at

night.

5. In case it rains, the basketball game will be cancelled.

---

62 1. I will write letters to you as long as I have free time.

2. You may get a gift as long as you attend the meeting.

3. As long as you agree to design the house for me, I don't mind how much money you charge.

4. As far as I know, Tim is a man of his word.

5. As far as I am concerned, there is nothing more important than health.

---

63 1. Work hard, and you will succeed.

2. Hurry up, or you will be late for school.

3. Get some sleep, or else you will be very tired tomorrow.

4. Finish the work right now. Otherwise, you will lose the chance of being promoted.

5. One more effort, and you will achieve your goal.

Exercises

I. 1. should 2. But, for

3. were 4. were, for

II. 1.C 2.C 3.C 4.D 5.A 6.C 7.C 8.D

Unit 10

64 1. I am as stubborn as my father.

2. Frank hasn't been to as/so many countries as his brother has.

---

65 1. The housing prices have risen twice as high as ten years ago.

2. He promised to raise my salary by quarter as much as it is.

3. This jeep is three times more expensive than that car.

4. The gym is ten times the size of the classroom.

5. This swimming pool is half the length of that one.

---

66 1. My mother is not so much a wife as a maid at home.

2. I lay down not so much to sleep as to ponder.

3. It counts not so much what you say as what you do.

4. The patient cannot so much as remember his own address.

5. Kevin went abroad without so much as informing his family.

---

67 1. This is the same watch as I bought in Paris.

2. This is the same watch that Cindy showed me.

3. You have made the same mistake as you did last time.

4. Annie was born on the same date as Ben was.

68

1. He is a pop singer as well as a teacher.

2. I as well as Jeri am wrong.

3. His idea is perfect in theory as well as in practice.

4. As early as the 14th century, Rome was a big city.

5. After the fire, the company is as good as ruined.

69

1. The greedier one is, the more one loses.

2. The higher we climb up, the farther we see.

3. The colder the weather (is), the more difficult our life (will be).

4. I love her all the more for her shortcomings.

5. He is none the happier for being very rich.

70

1. I would rather stay home than go out in such weather.

2. She would rather travel to America alone.

3. He would rather not take the plane to Europe.

4. Ken would sooner be hungry than eat what his sister cooked.

5. He would as soon quit the job at once as apologize.

71

1. My grandpa can read Japanese, much more speak Japanese.

2. My grandma cannot speak Chinese, much less write it.

3. My mother enjoys writing music, not to mention listening to music.

4. My brother dare not stamp on cockroaches, not to speak of killing people.

5. Tom doesn't respect his parents at all, let alone be grateful to them.

72

1. Jill's mother is beautiful, and what's more, she's very graceful.

2. This morning I got up late; what's worse, I had five tests today.

73

1. We know better than to expect a kindness from an enemy.

2. Employees know better than to quarrel with their employers.

3. You should know better at your age.

4. Adam agreed on our request in the beginning, but he thought better of it.

5. Don't spend more than you can help.

74

1. A hippo is no more a horse than a donkey is.

2. I cannot play tennis any more than you can.

3. He is not more careful than you are.

75

1. No less than one thousand people were killed in the earthquake.

2. Mr. Wang earns no less than five

million dollars a year.

3. It is not more than five minutes' walk from my home to school.

4. We have to stay at the airport not less than three hours.

5. You'll wait for me not more than half an hour.

76
1. To me, nothing is so important as time.

2. Shirley is more beautiful than any other girl at our school.

3. Speeding driving is the most dangerous.

4. No other city in Taiwan is so large as Taipei.

77
1. The new colleague is senior to us.

2. My English ability is inferior to my brother's.

3. Kathy is junior to me by one year.

4. The quality of Carol's camera is superior to that of Jennifer's.

Exercises

I. 1. not, much 2. no, less
3. than, any, other, city 4. no, less

II. 1. can no more play the violin than Jack can
2. is superior to the service of

III. 1.A 2.A 3.C 4.C 5.C
6.B 7.A 8.C 9.D 10.D

Unit 11

78
1. The rich are not always happy.

2. Food that looks good does not necessarily taste good.

3. It was quite difficult to defeat the boxer, but not absolutely impossible.

4. She is not exactly that stupid.

5. Not every student likes this teacher.

79
1. The couple never meet without quarreling.

Whenever the couple meet, they quarrel.

2. I never look at this picture without thinking of the days when we were young.

Every time I look at this picture, I think of the days when we were young.

3. Father never sees me without losing his temper.

Whenever Father sees me, he loses his temper.

80
1. My uncle is not a businessman but a scholar.

2. Ken said, "I'm not a citizen of China or Taiwan, but of the world."

3. What matters is not what you do but how you do it.

4. Jenny is popular not because of her pretty looks but because of her good personality.

81
1. We cannot be too careful when

choosing a school for kids.

2. I cannot thank you too much for your kindness.

3. We cannot overvalue the importance of peace.

4. One cannot make too many friends.

5. We cannot emphasize the importance of learning English too much.

---

82 1. Jessica is the last person to make such a mistake.

2. It is far from my intention to help you.

3. Mr. Chen's reply is far from satisfaction.

4. I think that he is anything but a loyal man.

5. You should be free from blame.

Exercises

I. 1. not, necessarily 2. anything, but

   3. cannot, be 4. far, from 5. but, for

II. 1.A 2.B 3.A 4.C 5.B

Unit 12

83 1. Even if Bill said so, we still didn't believe him.

2. I will complete the report even if it takes me all day.

3. Even though I tried, I couldn't change her mind.

4. In spite of her sadness, she pretended to be happy.

5. For all her fame and wealth, she is still

unhappy.

---

84 1. Young as she is, she is very wise.

2. Fast though you read, you can't finish the book in a day.

3. Woman as she is, she is brave on the battlefield.

4. Old as my grandfather is, he is still active.

---

85 1. Whether you win or lose, you will learn a lot from the game.

2. Whether the task is easy or difficult, do your best.

3. Whether you like it or not, you have to learn English.

4. I don't know whether the news is true or not.

5. Believe it or not, Brenda was fired today.

---

86 1. However tired I may be, I have to do my homework.

2. Whoever may object, I will marry Emily.

3. Wherever she may go, she is welcomed.

4. However hard he may try, he won't make it.

5. Whichever you may choose, I'll pay for it.

---

87 1. It is true that she is clever, but she has

no common sense.

2. It is true that he is rich, but he is very stingy.

3. No doubt his idea is great, but I don't think it is practicable.

4. Truly, it is very hot this year, but it is not as humid as usual.

5. This house is inexpensive, to be sure, but I don't want to buy it.

88　1. There is little wine left, if any.

2. There are few people, if any, who are concerned about air pollution.

3. He is seldom, if ever, late for appointments.

4. We can make a faster journey by taking a plane, if not a cheap one.

5. I bought the cheaper doll, if not my favorite one.

Exercises

　I. 1. as/though, but, Though/Although

　　2. spite, all, Even, though 3. may

　II. 1.A 2.C 3.D 4.C 5.C

Unit 13

89　1. We must do our best so that we may win.

2. You should read English newspapers every day so that your English may improve.

3. The campers made a fire so that they might make dinner.

4. Our teacher made a new rule last week so as to prevent cheating.

5. He went to Paris for the purpose of studying painting.

90　1. I stepped aside lest I should be in the old lady's way.

2. Please don't turn on the TV lest you should wake up the baby.

3. Remember to take a map with you in case you get lost.

4. Don't get close to the cage for fear that the tiger might bite you.

5. I get up early every day for fear of missing the train.

91　1. Sandra speaks so fast that we can't follow her.

2. It was such a fine day yesterday that we went on a picnic.

3. He is so foolish as to tell her the truth.

4. She is so sick that she can't work.

5. This is such an expensive car that Larry can't buy it.

92　1. This glass of water is too hot for me to drink.

2. The car is too far away for me to see.

3. The box is too heavy for him to carry alone.

4. She was too shocked to speak.

5. I came home too late to watch my favorite TV show yesterday.

93

1. My car broke down, so that I walked to work this morning.

2. Becky called her parents, so that they knew she had arrived at the dormitory.

3. My father used to work hard while young, and so he made a big fortune.

4. I took a taxi so that I might attend the class on time.

5. He was so tired that he couldn't concentrate on his homework.

94

1. I worked hard only to fail again.

2. We went to the North Pole last year, only to find nothing exciting.

3. The boy has spent two hours on homework, only to finish half of it.

4. I awoke to find myself lying in the hospital.

5. She decided never to return home unless she earned one million dollars when she was twenty.

95

1. To Henry's surprise, his daughter decided to marry a man who is twenty years older than her.

2. To my astonishment, she suddenly burst out laughing in public.

3. To our joy, the host team won the game yesterday.

4. To my great relief/Much to my relief, all the problems have been solved.

5. Much to her sorrow, her grandfather died last week.

Exercises

I. 1.A 2.B 3.D 4.B 5.C 6.B 7.C 8.D

Unit 14

96

1. I prefer tea to coffee. So does Tom.

2. Lucy is a college student. So am I.

3. I cannot speak Japanese. Neither/Nor can he.

4. A: You seem to be a musician. B: So I am.

97

1. She demanded that the newspaper make a public apology.

2. The king ordered that the soldier be put to death.

3. In the last discussion, I insisted that he resign as chairperson.

98

1. Why not ask her if she wants to dine out?

2. How come you didn't ask him for help?

3. "Don't park your car here!" "Why not?"

4. "Let's accept her proposal." "Why not?"

5. Why was it (that) he deserted his wife and children?

99

1. Leave the matter as it is.

2. Don't quarrel any longer. The situation is bad enough as it is.

3. If I were a police officer, I would arrest him now. But as it is, I cannot do this.

4. The law, as it is, is not strict enough.

5. Alice, concentrating on scientific research, as it were, is a modern Madame Curie.

---

100 1. How much money <u>on earth/in the world</u> do you need?

2. Why <u>on earth/in the world</u> did they yell at you yesterday?

3. Where <u>on earth/in the world</u> is Dr. Martin going?

4. This is the very puppy that I brought home yesterday.

5. I did forget about your invitation.

---

101 1. You can cry if you want to.

2. There are all sizes of boats. Some are big, and some small.

3. Comic books not only appeal to children but to adults.

4. Though (being) very poor, they led a happy life.

5. Mr. White's daughter, Sonia, got married yesterday.

Exercises

I. 1. nor, am 2. as, they, are

3. Why, not

II. 1.D 2.B 3.C

索引：依照字母順序

A

All + S + can do is (to) V...	p.69
All (that) + S + have/has to do is (to) V...	**p.68**
(all) the + 比較級 + for/because...	p.101
All + S + V + is that...	p.69
...and...are two different things	p.14
and that + 副詞/副詞片語	p.16
...and not...	p.115
anything but...	p.118
as + Adj/Adv + as + N/子句...	**p.95**
as + S + V + 比較級, S + V + 比較級	p.101
as early as...	p.100
as good as...	p.100
as it is	**p.142**
as it were	p.143
as many/much as	p.107
as/so far as...	p.90
as/so far as...be concerned	p.90
as/so long as...	**p.90**
...as/though + S + V	**p.122**
awake to find...	p.135
...as well as...	**p.99**

B

be accustomed to + N/V-ing	**p.58**
be anxious/eager to V	p.36
be apt/liable/prone to V	p.36
be busy (in) + V-ing	p.61
be dedicated to + N/V-ing	p.59
be free to V	p.36

be in the habit of + V-ing	**p.57**
be likely to V	**p.35**
be opposed to + N/V-ing	p.59
be ready to V	p.36
be superior to...	**p.109**
be sure to V	p.36
be to V	**p.28**
be used to + N/V-ing	**p.58**
Being + V-en	p.44
but for...	**p.85**
by oneself	**p.15**
by the time...	p.79

C

cannot but + 原形 V	**p.32**
cannot choose but + 原形 V	p.32
cannot have + V-en	p.22
cannot help + V-ing	p.32
cannot help but + 原形 V	p.32
cannot...too many/much...	p.116
cannot...too...	**p.116**
come near + V-ing	p.61
come to V	**p.33**
considering...	p.46
could have + V-en	p.22

DEFG

'd like to	p.23
despite...	p.121
do nothing but + 原形 V	p.32
do/does/did + 原形 V	p.144
...enough to V	p.37
even if/though	**p.121**

every time...	**p.79**	How about + N/V-ing?	p.55
far from...	p.118	How come...?	p.142
feel like + N/V-ing	**p.56**	How I wish...	p.87
find difficulty (in) + V-ing	p.61	How long does it take to V?	p.5
find it + Adj/N + to V	**p.2**	**however...may...**	**p.124**
for all	p.121		
for fear (that)...should/might/would...	p.130		

I

for fear of + V-ing	p.130	If + S + were to + 原形 V..., S + 過去式助動詞	
for oneself	p.15	(should/would/could/might) + 原形 V...	
for the purpose of + N/V-ing	p.129		p.83
frankly speaking	**p.45**	if anything...	p.127
free from...	p.118	**If it were not for..., ...**	**p.84**
generally speaking	p.46	if not...	p.127
get + O + V-en	p.49	**If only...**	**p.86**
get to V	p.33	**If...should...**	**p.83**
grow up to be...	p.135	in case...	p.89, 131
		in itself	p.15
		in other words	p.17

H

		in spite of...	p.121
had better + 原形 V	**p.20**	in + V-ing	p.53
have + the + 抽象名詞 + to V	**p.36**	...is different from...	p.14
have + O + V-en	**p.49**	**...is one thing and...is another**	**p.14**
have difficulty (in) + V-ing	p.61	**It doesn't matter...whether...**	**p.7**
have good reason to V	p.21	It follows that...	p.4
have something to oneself	p.15	It goes without saying that...	p.5
have something/nothing to do with...	**p.34**	it is impossible...to...too...	p.116
have the boldness to V	p.37	It is no use + V-ing	p.2
have the courage to V	p.37	It is said that...	p.4
have the folly to V	p.37	**It is time + 假設法過去式**	**p.87**
have the fortune to V	p.37	**It is true (that)...but...**	**p.125**
have the kindness to V	p.37	**It is...for...to V**	**p.1**
Having + V-en	p.44	It is...of...to V	p.1
Having been + V-en	p.44	**It is...since...**	**p.78**
hinder...from + V-ing	p.60		

It is...that...	**p.8**
It makes no difference whether...	p.8
It occurs to + sb + that...	**p.6**
It seems/appears that...	**p.4**
It strikes + sb + that...	p.6
It takes...to V	**p.5**

JKL

judging from...	p.46
keep busy (in) + V-ing	p.61
keep...from + V-ing	p.60
know better than to V	**p.105**
lest...(should) + 原形 V	**p.130**
let alone	p.103
little..., if any	**p.126**
look forward to + N/V-ing	p.58

M

make it a rule to V	p.3, 57
make oneself understood	**p.50**
manage to V	p.34
may as well not...	p.20
may as well...	p.20
may well + 原形 V	p.21
may/might as well A as B	p.20
may/might have + V-en	**p.21**
more than one can help	p.105
more...than...	p.97
much more...	**p.103**
must have + V-en	p.22

N

need not have + V-en	p.22

Neither/Nor + 助動詞/be 動詞 + S	p.139
never fail to V	p.114
never to...	p.135
never...without + V-ing	**p.114**
no...but...	**p.67**
no less than...	**p.107**
no more...than...	**p.106**
no sooner...than...	**p.75**
none the + 比較級 + for/because...	p.101
not always...	**p.113**
not because...but because...	p.115
not even...	p.97
not less than...	p.107
not merely...but...as well	p.99
no more than...	p.107
not more than...	p.107
not more...than...	p.106
not only...but also...	p.99
not so much...as...	**p.97**
not so much as...	p.97
not to mention...	p.39, 103
not to speak of...	p.39, 103
Not until...	p.77
not...but...	**p.115**
not...long before...	**p.76**
not...till/until...	**p.77**
not...without + V-ing	**p.114**
Nothing is so...as...	**p.108**

OPR

Oh, that...	p.87
on condition (that)...	p.89
On + V-ing	**p.53**

one..., and the other(s)...	**p.11**	Suppose/Supposing (that)...	**p.88**
one another	p.14		
one...another...the other(s)...	p.13	**T**	
...only to...	**p.134**	take it for granted that...	p.3
or else	p.91	taking...into consideration	p.46
or	p.91	talking/speaking of...	p.46
otherwise	p.91	that is (to say)	p.17
ought to have + V-en	p.22	**that of...**	**p.16**
prevent...from + V-ing	**p.59**	that...this...	p.12
prove to V	p.33	**the + 比較級..., the + 比較級...**	**p.100**
...rather than...	p.97	The best + S + can do is (to) V...	p.69
		the former..., the latter...	p.12
		the last...to V	**p.117**
S		(the) last time...	p.79
see/feel/listen to/watch + O + 原形 V	**p.31**	(the) next time...	p.79
seem + to V	p.4	**the one..., and the other...**	**p.11**
seem to have + V-en	**p.30**	**the same...as...**	**p.98**
seldom/rarely..., if ever	p.127	the very + N	p.144
should have + V-en	p.22	**There be + S + 分詞**	**p.47**
So + 助動詞/be 動詞 + S	**p.139**	There is no use + V-ing	p.54
so that...may/can/will...	**p.129**	**There is no + V-ing**	**p.54**
so to speak	p.39	There is nothing like + N/V-ing	p.55
so...as to...	p.37, 132	think better of...	p.105
so...that...	**p.131**	**This is why...**	**p.70**
..., so that...	**p.133**	This/That is how...	p.70
so-called	p.66	This/That is the reason (that)...	p.70
some..., and/but others...	**p.13**	This/That is the way (that)...	p.70
stick to + N/V-ing	p.59	those...these...	p.12
stop...from + V-ing	p.59	...times + 所有格 + N	p.96
strange/needless to say	p.38	...times + 比較級 + than...	p.96
such as...	p.67	**...times as...as**	**p.95**
such...as...	**p.67**	...times the + N + of + 所有格的受格	p.96
such...that...	p.131	to be brief	p.38
suggest that + S + (should) + 原形 V	**p.140**		

to be frank	p.38
to begin with	p.38
to do someone justice	p.38
to make a long story short	p.38
to make matters worse	p.38
to one's regret/shock/joy	p.136
to one's surprise	**p.136**
to put it differently	p.17
to say nothing of	p.38, 103
to sum up	p.38
to tell the truth	**p.38**
too...to...	**p.132**
turn out to V	p.34

UVW

Upon + V-ing	**p.53**
used to V	**p.19**
what + N	**p.71**
What do you say to + V-ing?	p.61
What I am	**p.65**
what makes matter worse	p.104
what one does	p.65
what one has	p.65
what we call	**p.66**
What/Where/How/When + on earth...?	**p.143**
What/Where/When/Why/How...+ to V	**p.27**
what's better	p.104
what's more	**p.104**
what's worse	p.104
When it comes to + N/V-ing	**p.60**
whether...or...	**p.123**
Who/What...+ is/was it that...?	p.9
..., who/whom/which...	**p.72**

Why is/was it (that)...?	p.142
Why not...?	**p.141**
with + O + Adj/Adv/介系詞片語	p.48
with + O + 分詞	**p.47**
with a view to...	p.129
with all	p.121
with an eye to...	p.129
without so much as + V-ing	p.98
without...	**p.85**
Would (that)...	p.87
would as soon...as...	p.102
would like + sb + to V	p.23
would like to V	**p.23**
would rather not...	p.102
would rather...than...	**p.102**
would sooner...than...	p.102
Would to God that...	p.87
Would you like...?	p.23
Would/Do you mind + V-ing?	**p.55**

Others

分詞構句	**p.43, 44**
命令句 + **and/or...**	**p.91**
省略句	**p.145**
感官/使役動詞 + O + 原形 V	**p.31**
不完全及物動詞 + it...for + 人 + to V	p.3

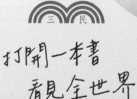

國家圖書館出版品預行編目資料

Key Sentence Structures 100：關鍵句型100／郭慧敏編
著.——三版一刷.——臺北市：三民，2023
面；　公分.——（英語Make Me High系列）

ISBN 978–957–14–7380–2　（平裝）
1. 英語 2. 句法

805.169　　　　　　　　　　　　　111000560

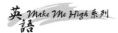

英語 Make Me High 系列

Key Sentence Structures 100：關鍵句型 100

編 著 者	郭慧敏
發 行 人	劉振強
出 版 者	三民書局股份有限公司
地　　址	臺北市復興北路 386 號 (復北門市)
	臺北市重慶南路一段 61 號 (重南門市)
電　　話	(02)25006600
網　　址	三民網路書店 https://www.sanmin.com.tw
出版日期	初版一刷 2005 年 4 月
	三版一刷 2023 年 8 月
書籍編號	S805280
I S B N	978-957-14-7380-2